The Sign
of the Tooth

A New Sherlock Holmes Mystery

By Craig Stephen Copland

Published by:

Conservative Growth

1101 30th Street NW, Ste. 500

Washington, DC 20007

Cover design by Rita Toews

ISBN-10:   1981377727

ISBN-13:978-1981377725

Dedication

To the wonderful friends and colleagues with whom I had the
joy of working during my many visits to Sri Lanka.

Contents

Acknowledgments

I discovered The Adventures of Sherlock Holmes while a student at Scarlett Heights Collegiate Institute in Toronto. My English teachers – Bill Stratton, Norm Oliver, and Margaret Tough – inspired me to read and write. I shall be forever grateful to them.

The plot of this novella is inspired by Arthur Conan Doyle's Sherlock Holmes Mystery, *The Sign of Four*. Your enjoyment of this book will be enhanced by a quick re-read of that intriguing story.

My dearest and best friend, Mary Engelking, read all drafts, helped with whatever historical and geographical accuracy was required, and offered insightful recommendations for changes to the narrative structure, characters, and dialogue.

Thanks also to Ms. Hajara Jesuri of Kandy, Sri Lanka, a talented online research assistant, for her invaluable contributions to the accurate setting of this story in Sri Lanka.

For the very idea of writing a new Sherlock Holmes mystery, I thank the Bootmakers, the Sherlock Holmes Society of Toronto. The reader's enjoyment of this novella will be greatly enhanced by re-reading *The Sign of the Four*, the original Sherlock Holmes story that has inspired this one.

Chapter One
The Bored Consultant

Lizzie Borden took an ax
And gave her mother forty whacks.
When she saw what she had done,
She gave her father forty-one.

"Holmes," I said one morning, "you must take a look at this latest on Lizzie."

The *Illustrated Times* had a ghastly sketch of the young Sunday School teacher hacking away at her mother's head with the caption "How She Might Have Done It." It was positively gruesome.

"Here, Holmes. Come take a look."

Sherlock Holmes glared across the room as I expected he would and in his surliest voice muttered, "You know perfectly well that I am not the least bit interested in lurid stories that the English press copies from the even more lurid American press. Kindly do not visit any more of those stories upon me."

"But Holmes," I continued. "If you will not look at the picture then read this. *The Telegraph* is saying that Miss Borden collapsed and fainted in the courtroom, and it was caused by the bringing of the severed heads of her mother and father as evidence. The story is utterly fascinating."

I was being deliberately provocative. My good friend, the brilliant detective whose mind never ceased its marvelous efforts once set upon the scent of a case, had been despondent for days. Nothing of interest had come across the doorstep of 221B Baker Street in several weeks, and I feared that he would resort yet again to his terrible dependence on pharmaceutical injections for no other reason than to relieve the boredom.

"Watson," he remonstrated. "Must I say again that I am not interested in the latest scandal from across the pond? That is entirely enough."

Like most Englishmen, including, I confess, yours truly, Holmes's could not find a single good word to say about America while all the time being inwardly envious and jealous of the opportunities that were enjoyed by all, even amateur detectives, in the colony that got away.

"Ahh," I said, ignoring him and continuing to read aloud. "The line to be taken by the defending attorney is unique and indeed quite daring. He is presenting several doctors and clergymen who will testify under oath that the female brain and indeed the female constitution as a whole is biologically – did you get that Holmes? *Biologically* – incapable of such a violent and bloody crime. What do you think of that, Holmes?"

He said nothing. He rose from his chair, approached me and removed the newspaper from my hands and read the story. As he did, he slowly shook his head.

"Oh what fools these mortals be, Watson," he muttered. "Have they completely forgotten the Amazons? Three thousand years ago they were impaling men on spears and hacking off their limbs. Our earnest suffragettes are telling us that women are equal to men in all possible ways, and they are entirely correct. This line of defense is pathetic. Even from the details given in the London press, I can see enormous gaping holes in the case presented by the prosecution. Had they any ability whatsoever in scientific deduction this woman would have been set free weeks ago."

"Oh. You don't say. I gather you have been following the story all along?"

"Only when I have felt the pain of utter mental stagnation, when I have been suffocated by the dull routine of existence. I created my role in society so that I could devote my mind to the solving of the most intricate problems and match wits with the most diabolical of criminals. And now I am faced with yet another empty day. So empty that even a banal item about Lizzie Borden brings a tiny serving of relief."

"Very well, Holmes," said I. "If you are going to be an unofficial detective..."

"A consulting detective. The only one in the world," he interjected.

"Fine. A consulting detective then. You are still dependent on cases walking across your threshold, but if the real detectives do their job halfways decently, there will be times when there are none left over for you."

"My dear friend," he said, and I sensed the annoyance in his voice, "I do not live on leftovers, as you suggest. I am consulted on cases when Lestrade, Gregson or Anderson find themselves to be in over their heads, which by the way happens rather often, and my peculiar powers are called for."

I had expected this protest to grow into a tirade, but suddenly his countenance softened as he looked out from our bay window down onto Baker Street.

"Speaking of Lestrade, he has just arrived in his private carriage."

"Really, Holmes. I did not know that Scotland Yard was now providing private carriages for their Inspectors."

"Of course, they are not, but the imbeciles over there decided that they wished to be secretive about their movements. So they purchased a dozen identical unmarked carriages with dark curtains. They are so bland and featureless that you can tell them from any other carriage in London a block away. Ahh ... but that is not Lestrade's leg emerging. It is a fine and shapely leg of a young lady."

"Oh. Is it now?" I said as I pushed aside the curtain from the other end of the window.

"Yes. And she is walking directly toward our door which means that she is not yet another of those pitiful young things that have pathetic affairs of the heart, and who walk back and forth several times, trying to make up their little minds, before finally knocking on my door."

When he spoke like this, I instinctively responded in anger. "The affairs of a young woman's heart are neither pathetic nor pitiful Holmes! Have you no feeling in that brain of yours at all?"

He was a little taken back at my admonition. "Oh, very well then, doctor. But you cannot deny that they are frightfully boring."

I was about to make such a denial forcefully, but Mrs. Hudson entered the room and announced, "Miss Mary Morstan, gentlemen."

Miss Morstan entered the room with a firm step and an aura of quiet confidence. When she removed her bonnet, a cascade of flaxen tresses fell to her shoulders. She was well-dressed, and her clothes had the crisp freshness of having been recently purchased on the High Street. Her eyes were utterly arresting. With such light hair, one would never have expected such dark eyes. So dark that had they been all I had seen of her I would have judged her to be gypsy. Her features, though fair, were not the aquiline sharply cut ones of the British Isles but softer and more rounded, almost child-like, and perfectly balanced. I have never looked upon a face to which I was so immediately drawn. As she took the seat that Sherlock Holmes had motioned her to, I could see a faint tremble in her lip. In spite of her radiance and loveliness, she was inwardly upset, and I had to restrain my instinctive response to place my arm around her shoulders and assure her that she was among friends who would protect her.

Using two hands, she removed her handbag from her shoulder and put it on the floor. Before either Holmes or I could say a word, Mrs. Hudson walked over to the young woman and placed her hand on her back in a motherly fashion. "A cup of tea, dearie? It will help you relax. And don't be intimidated by these two oddballs. Their bark is much worse than their bite, and they are quite good at whatever it is they do."

Miss Morstan smiled at Mrs. Hudson. "Thank you. A spot of tea would help me compose myself. Thank you." Mrs. Hudson departed but not without first giving a hard look at both Holmes and me that promised a rap on our knuckles if we were less than considerate to the young woman.

Holmes began. "Allow me to offer my condolences first on having to endure a long interview with those fools over at Scotland Yard, but more so on your recent loss and bereavement. The pain of these things, though unbearable at the time, does eventually pass. The fact that you have come into a goodly inheritance as a result of your father's service under the Raj will help to improve the process. The recent increase in the price of gold will no doubt speed the rate of improvement, and you will likely to be able to say goodbye to your role as a governess, even though you adore your little charges and are loved joyfully in return."

Most young clients to whom Holmes delivered his practiced assessment react in shock and wonder. Miss Morstan did no such thing. She quietly accepted her tea from Mrs. Hudson, and then looked directly at Holmes and shrugged. "Inspector Lestrade certainly has you pegged Mr. Holmes."

"I beg your pardon, miss?" said Holmes. He was apparently not expecting this response.

"Inspector Lestrade told me on no uncertain terms that I was not to tell you that I had been meeting with him but that you would most likely know that all the same. He also said that you would tell me all sorts of things about myself but not to be surprised because it was your way of showing off. He said that you were the oddest bloke in town — but brilliant —

and if I could live with your peculiarities that you could help me."

I could not resist asking her, "Did Lestrade indeed say that Sherlock Holmes was 'an odd bloke?'"

"No. Truthfully, he said 'Frankly miss, Sherlock Holmes is positively weird and endlessly annoying' but I did not want to be rude, so I softened his words because I need your help."

"But," I pressed, "did he actually admit that Sherlock Holmes was 'brilliant?'"

"No. Truthfully, he called him an *imbecile savant*. But he insisted that I meet with you all the same."

"Enough of Lestrade," said Holmes, who did not appear to be enjoying this exchange. "State your case."

I had had sufficient inward chuckles to last me the day and seeing that Holmes had returned to being a detective, a consulting detective I must not forget, I felt it appropriate for me to leave the room. "I assure you miss, that he is indeed truly brilliant, even if all those other things are true as well," I said, with a departing bow of my head.

"Oh, please no. Please stay. The Inspector said that I should ask you to help as well because even though you were not at all brilliant you were always kind and considerate and a necessary balance to Sherlock Holmes."

I smiled and took my seat in the empty chair, not entirely sure if I had been complemented or otherwise.

Chapter Two
The Statement of the Case

"**I** may as well start," she began, "with what you already know. As I entered this room, I saw you look at my shoes, and you no doubt observed that while they are brand new, they are black and plain and terribly unstylish, the sort that a young woman would buy only if she were required to participate in a funeral. I have come into some money very recently and, therefore, the new dress. And my handbag is extremely heavy; you could tell that from the way it bulged, the strain on the shoulder strap, and my needing two hands to lift it. So, you deduced that I have something very heavy in it, and as I am unlikely to be carrying rocks around London, it is more likely that there is gold therein.

"I am of mixed race as you observed by the color of my

eyes and the shape of my features and yes, my father, Captain Robert Morstan, was in the Royal Engineers and served in Ceylon. My mother was Ceylonese. As to my being a governess, you are also correct, but I am not sure how you deduced that fact. I am an unmarried woman in my mid-twenties, and it is a reasonable guess to make as to my vocation, but there would be other possibilities, so I am not sure how you landed on governess."

"Ah," said Holmes, looking a little disappointed that his revelations had not exactly been considered miraculous. "On the left side of your skirt, you have a smudge with a spot of granular material. There is a similar one on the other side but a little lower down. Such residue is a telltale sign of a child's face, having climbed down from the breakfast table while still covered with milk and porridge, and giving an affectionate embrace to his or her much-loved governess. That there are two at different heights indicates two children, close in age. They appear to be very fond of you, in a sloppy sort of way."

She smiled. "Yes they are and I of them. I shall miss them. The reason for my departure from that service is related to the reason for my being here."

"Yes. Enough of wet-faced children," said Holmes. "You were stating your case."

"I am here because my father and his closest friend both died within the past three weeks and I believe that they were murdered."

"Indeed, and the dates?" queried Holmes.

"My father two weeks past. His dearest friend, Major John Sholto, a week ago. Both were elderly men in their eighties and had lived long and full lives, and no one seemed surprised when my father was found dead in his study. The doctor said it was a heart failure. No medical examination was performed since he was of advanced age. When the major died a week later, it was agreed that the stress of losing his friend had put a toll on his heart and he passed on as well."

"Those are reasonable explanations," I said. "When men are that old their hearts cannot last much longer. Why do you suspect foul play?"

"Both my father and Major Sholto were old but were still in robust health. There had been no signs of weak hearts in either of them. But that is not the reason for my suspicion. My father had finished his supper and had gone to his study. When the maid brought him his evening tea an hour later, she found him dead at his desk. She tried to shake him and reported that although his body was still warm, all his limbs had gone stiff as boards. Rigor mortis had completely set in."

"That is very unusual," I noted, "but there could be reasons for it. I am not aware of any, but strange things do happen especially with men who have served in the tropics. No telling what unknown pathogens might have entered their systems."

She nodded. "That is what the local doctor said. But a week later Major Sholto died, also in the evening after supper, also in his study, and also with immediate stiffening of his body."

Holmes was now sitting forward. His hands were held in front of his chin and his fingertips pressed together. "That is most certainly a very strange coincidence and although suspicious, does not demand that foul play is the only possible explanation."

"And then this, in yesterday's paper," she said, handing Holmes a clipping. He read it and gave it to me. It ran:

Death of a Student

Oxford. Local police report that the body of a Master Dharmarathna Gunawardhana, a medical student from Ceylon, who was studying at the University, was found in the library yesterday evening. No known cause has been given, and we are awaiting the report of the coroner. The library cleaning staff who found him shortly after the closing hour are reported to have said that he must have been dead for some time as rigor mortis had already set in. There is some confusion on this matter as a fellow student, Master Chandrarathna Wijekulaseriya, also from Ceylon, has been quoted as saying that he had chatted with the deceased just before the closing of the library. Two inspectors from Scotland Yard are investigating, but no report has yet been released. The University has stated that the lad will be greatly missed not only as he was a capable young man on his way to becoming a doctor, but also for his skills on the cricket field. He had excelled at the sport since his days as a scholar at Trinity College in Kandy. Messages of condolence may be sent care of the Central Telegraph in Kandy, Ceylon.

"This young man's father had been a friend of my father

in Ceylon, and after his classes were over for the term, he had been helping my father and Major Sholto on their latest project."

Holmes had dropped his hands, and they were firmly clasping the arms of his chair. His eyes had become focused on the young woman's face. "When an unusual event happens once, it is happenstance. When it happens twice, it is a curious coincidence. When it happens a third time, it is a criminal conspiracy. You, my dear young lady, might also be in danger. I trust you are taking appropriate precautions."

"That is why I went to the police, sir. But that is not why they, as well as another party, sent me to see you. I believe, although they did not tell me outright, that it was because of the project on which my father, the Major, and young Dharmy were working."

"And what might that have been. Tell us," said Holmes impatiently.

She nodded. I noticed her hands twitching as she twisted her handkerchief. Had Holmes overbearing presence not been directly between us I would have placed my hand on top of hers and told her to take her time, but I refrained and withheld my annoyance with my friend.

"It might be best if I were to start back a few years ago," she said after composing herself. "My story requires some explaining."

"It is always good to have a complete set of data on which to make insights and judgments," said Holmes brusquely. "Please give us all the pertinent facts, miss, and do get on with it. We do not have all day."

"Holmes, honestly!" I sputtered. "The young lady is under duress. Have some consideration."

"Oh, very well. I correct myself. My colleague, Dr. Watson may have all day, but I do not. Please get on with it."

Instead of looking at him with a hurtful expression, she turned to me and gave a wan but warm smile.

"It is quite all right, doctor. The Inspector warned me about his behavior. He said 'Holmes would forget his manners in front of the Queen if his brain were already lost in the plot of the crime.' He said to take it as a good sign that he was already at work on my behalf."

Holmes harrumphed. She smiled at him and began her story.

"My father studied at the University of Edinburgh and upon graduation joined the Royal Engineers. He was posted to Ceylon and put to work building the railroad from the port of Trincomalee up to Kandy. His fellow engineer was John Sholto, also a Scotsman, who had done his studies in Glasgow, and they became good friends and worked alongside each other. Near to the end of his posting my father was injured and was released from the regiment with a small pension. He would have returned home, but he had no real family back in Scotland, and his friends were all in his regiment. He had also fallen in love with the island of Ceylon and particularly with the city of Kandy. He thought it a magical place. It happened that some missionaries from the Church of England had started a school there, Trinity College, and they were in need of someone to teach the boys their maths. They invited my father to join the staff of the college. He did and taught the boys for the next thirty years. He was enraptured with his calling, with the Spice Island, and with the art, history, and culture of Kandy. In addition to teaching, he coached the boys in cricket, and he became quite the scholar and published several books and monographs about the Kingdom of Kandy.

"John Sholto, who I called my Uncle John although we are not related, continued to serve in the Engineers and was promoted to the rank of major. He returned to England, married, and set up a small estate near Norwood. He had two sons, twins, and provided his family with a good life, but he continued his close friendship with Father. They wrote to each other every week. He came to visit every second year, and he also became an amateur expert on the religion and history of Kandy. The two of them became a little team of scholars and had a small reputation in the Royal Society, but they were highly esteemed by the Ceylonese who lived in Kandy. You may know that Kandy was the last independent kingdom to fall to the British Empire. The Kandians are very attached to their unique history and very fond of those foreigners who choose to live there and learn about their special corner of heaven on earth.

"While he was teaching, my father lived on the college grounds and lived very frugally. He remained single, set his military pension and most of his salary aside, and shrewdly invested in the new tea gardens that were being opened far up in the highlands near Nuwara Eliya. He convinced Uncle John to do the same. Over time, their shares grew, and they became very wealthy men. He never let on and thought it unseemly for a man to flaunt his money, so he continued to live in his cottage and teach the boys maths and cricket. When he turned fifty-five years of age, he retired. To everyone's surprise, and I gather to some shock and outrage, he married my mother, who was twenty-five years his junior, a native of the island, and the college's accountant."

"Oh my," said I. "That must have caused quite a stir."

She laughed. It was good to see that her distress had lessened. "Not as much as you might think it would, doctor. There are many, many English soldiers, civil servants, and missionaries who have, as they say, 'gone native' and become attached to a dark-skinned woman of the sub-continent. Some took Indian and Ceylonese girls as their wives and countless more as their mistresses.

"I was born the following year. We Anglo-Indians, as our mongrel race is known. There are several million of us now We are, in the words of my father, an everlasting biological monument to the adultery of the British Raj."

"That is very endearing," said Holmes. "It has nothing to do with any crime. Please get back to the essentials."

"Of course, sir," she said and flashed a beautiful sparkling smile back at Holmes. "Even though my father was an older man he was a vigorous man and, being retired, had the freedom to go on countless adventures with his little girl. My childhood in the highlands of Ceylon was a fairy tale. Once a week my father and mother and I would rise before dawn and drive our carriage all the way to Nuwara Eliya. As the morning sun came over the tops of the hills, I would watch the sunlight bounce off of scores of silver waterfalls. As the mist rose off the tea gardens, we would hear the voices, the singing of the Ceylonese women as they walked along the rows of the tea plants plucking the leaves and tossing them back over their shoulders into the wicker buckets that were strapped to their backs. Up to a dozen women would work together, each with her own row, but walking in unison through the gardens and singing. We would stop along the way at a tea house and drink the tea that had been picked and roasted the day before, and it was the finest elixir on earth. Father used to say that all the good tea was consumed in India and Ceylon, that the second rate leaves were sent to England, and that the grounds off the floor were swept up, put into tea bags and sent to America, where they were as likely to throw it into the harbor as brew it properly.

"I became a bit of a scholar and learned the ancient Sinhala alphabet and the language, and could read and speak it rather fluently. Father and I chatted in that tongue just for fun at times.

"On our winter break, he took me on his hunting trips, even on three tiger hunts in India. During the summers, we would take a vacation to the seaside in Galle, or over to the beautiful white beaches at Batticaloa. It was as wonderful a childhood as I could ever dream of. It lasted for the first ten years of my life and then, to everyone's surprise, my mom being forty and dad sixty-five, mother found herself expecting a child. I could tell that they were very worried and, sadly, the result was tragic. Both my mother and my baby sister, Anne, died in childbirth. My father was utterly heartbroken. He tried to keep being cheerful for my sake, but he was never the same.

"When I was twelve we came back to England and settled in London. Father and the Major spent a great deal of time together, most of it at the British Museum where they continued their scholarly study about the Kingdom of Kandy and founded the Society for Kandian Research. The center of all Kandian culture, art, and religion, as you may know, is the Sri Dalada Maligawa, the Temple of the Tooth. Over one thousand years ago Princess Hemamali brought to Kandy the tooth of the Buddha. It has been kept and venerated since that time in the great golden temple that sits by Bogambara Lake. It is the very beating heart of Kandy. Father and Uncle John are, or I must say were, the experts in all of England concerning the Tooth of the Buddha. Every year they spent two months back in Kandy pursuing their research. And that, sirs, is the project on which they were working when they died or, I must say, were killed."

"The Tooth," I cried out. "The Tooth of the Buddha? You have read about this, Holmes, have you not?"

The story had been all over the Press for weeks now. After months of negotiations, the Tooth had been brought it to London. The priests had refused to let it leave the temple until they were promised thousands of pounds worth of temple renovations, and agreed that temple priests would accompany it and never let it leave their sight. It would soon be on display at the British Museum, and thousands were expected to queue up to see it.

The special exhibit, *The Wisdom Tooth of the Buddha*, was scheduled to open in five days. The relic of Gautama Buddha was every bit as important to his followers as the Shroud of Turin was to the Catholics. While an old molar was in itself hardly anything to get all excited about, the Foreign Office had gone all out to assemble a magnificent display of the wealthy artifacts of the Raj. It mattered not that some were from Rajasthan, some from Bihar, and many from Bangalore, as long as they looked spectacular and drew a constant crowd. Photographs of the citizenry of London, having removed their shoes and looking up in worshipful awe at the sacred tooth, would be distributed all over the empire, proving that the heart of the Empire and the heart of the average Englishman beat in unison with all of the dark-skinned subjects of Her Gracious Majesty.

"Hmm. Yes. I do recall seeing some mention in the press," said Holmes. "Struck me as more an exceptional propaganda coup for the Empire than an effort of scholarship. Having countless English blokes and nannies all oooing and aahhhing over it makes the Empire look as if we actually respect the superstitions and handcrafts of the benighted heathen. When, if fact, we do nothing of the sort."

"Oh, come come, Holmes. Must you always be so cynical?"

"When it comes to political spectacle, cynicism is not only rational, it is imperative," he snapped back at me. "Nevertheless, Miss Morstan, do you have any knowledge of what your father, the major, and the young Mr. Wiji … Mr. … ahh, Master Dharmy were doing as regards this special exhibit."

"No, I fear I do not. It was all rather secretive, and their conversations were very quiet. I do not live in the same house as my father any longer and only visited him on Saturdays. He generally did not work on those days and generously devoted the time to outings with me. Even though he was eighty years old, I was always his little girl." As she spoke, tears formed in her beautiful dark eyes and crept down her lovely face.

"It is unfortunate," said Holmes, "that your intellectual curiosity was non-existent and that you were content to be a governess, but it cannot be helped, and you will not be of much use along that line of investigation. Very well then, what have you brought in your bag?"

Again, instead of being offended, Miss Morstan smiled back at Holmes and sweetly replied, "I thought you would never ask."

She proceeded to reach into her large handbag and slowly extract and place on the table eight objects, all about the size of a fist. Each was wrapped in a black silk cloth, and she waited until the last one was on the table before returning to the first to untie the gold thread that held it together. I could see the vein in Holmes's left temple starting to throb as he waited in frustrated impatience for the ritual to be completed and the objects to be revealed. Miss Morstan went about her

18

task with apparent unrelenting concentration, but I suspected that she was playing a game of wits with Holmes and, as far as I could see, was winning this round. I felt myself growing fonder of her by the minute.

One by one the artifacts were exposed. Every one of them was a small statuette of the sitting Buddha, and every one in gleaming gold, yet each in a slightly different pose.

"Would you like to look at one more closely?" she said, looking up demurely at Holmes. It was all I could do not to break out laughing and shout, "Of course he would. He is dying to look at it. You are torturing him."

To his credit Holmes, with delicious difficulty, refrained from being rude and brusque and snatching one off the table. He nodded politely and replied, "Yes, my dear. I would. If you would be so kind as to hand me the first one."

Holmes received the statuette and bounced it for a moment in his hand. It was clearly a heavy little fellow. "This is heavy enough to be solid gold." He removed his glass from his pocket and began a careful examination. "I could not say without taking it to a jeweler, but it appears to be of at least eighteen karat, if not twenty. The carving is exquisite. There are hundreds of fine details. It must have taken weeks of painstaking work from a master carver to make this.

"Are they all the same weight?" he asked Miss Morstan.

"Yes," she replied. "There is nothing other than the changes in the pose of the Buddha to differentiate them from each other. Each one represents one of the eight paths of noble enlightenment."

"Remarkable," said Holmes. "Every one of these must be worth hundreds of pounds for the gold alone. I have no expertise in the precious art of Ceylon, but I imagine that if these were to be auctioned by Sotheby's they would fetch well over a thousand pounds a piece, and many times that figure for the full set. So please, Miss Morstan, how is it that you have come to have these in your possession?"

"The first one arrived the day following my father's funeral. Then one each weekday after that. After the eighth, they stopped. Each was carefully enclosed in a small wooden case with protective wrapping."

"And were there any notes or instructions?"

"There was one with the first. And then another one with the last one and I have no idea from whom they came."

She reached into her handbag and handed two folded pieces of paper to Sherlock Holmes. He unfolded it, read it and handed it to me.

June 3, 1902
On this day, you begin to receive your inheritance. Mine must wait another decade.
     With warmest regards,

"Your inheritance, Miss Morstan?" said Holmes. "Were you expecting something following the death of your father?"

"Yes, but nothing until after the estate had cleared probate, and even then it would be the shares in the tea gardens, not a set of precious golden carvings."

"When did you say your father died?"

"A fortnight ago."

"But this note is dated before that time. It is very unlikely that whoever sent it could have known that your father was going to die. Was there any other significance to that date, Miss Morstan? To the third of June, 1902?"

"It was my twenty-fifth birthday."

Holmes said nothing for a moment and then held up the second note. "I suppose I am required to congratulate the writer on his good judgment." He then read the note.

My dear Mary Morstan:

Your life is now in danger. I beg you please to seek the immediate protection of the police. You should also contact Mr. Sherlock Holmes at 221B Baker Street and ask for his help.

With deepest concern,

Holmes sat in silence for a moment and then turned abruptly to the young lady. "Very well, miss. I will take on your case and expect to receive no payment unless it is resolved to your satisfaction. Take these figurines of Mr. Buddha and immediately put them into a safe box in a bank. The Capital and County Bank is close by on Oxford Street just a block east of Baker Street. I suggest you go there. Now get yourself out of here and back to your sloppy-faced children. I have work to do. Go. Now. And leave those notes with us."

Miss Morstan smiled back at Holmes, packed her Buddhas back into her handbag, rose and walked toward the door. I moved quickly to open it for her. "I will see you to the street and fetch a cab," I said.

"Oh, Doctor Watson," she replied, with a radiant smile.

"That is entirely unnecessary, but I do thank you for your kindness." Then, lightly putting her hand on my forearm and with a hint of a twinkle in her eye, added, "I do believe the good Lord gave you not only a kind spirit but also a handsome face. It is a pity that you are covering so much of it with those silly mutton-chop whiskers and walrus's mustache." Then she turned and descended the stairs. I walked over to the window and watched until she had climbed safely into a cab.

Chapter Three
Mycroft

I then turned to Sherlock Holmes and in a firm voice said, "You really are an automaton — a calculating machine. There is something positively inhuman in you sometimes. Could you not display even a jot of consideration for the feelings of a young woman in distress."?

"My dear friend, I am considerate of my client's bank accounts, of keeping them from bankruptcy, prison, the gallows, and disastrous marriages. I am considerate of protecting their reputations even when they rightly deserved to be dragged through the mud. I am considerate of their property and even of rescuing their stupid children. I consider that those considerations are quite enough. I have neither the time nor the patience to consider their utterly unpredictable feelings."

"Holmes, you are wrong!" I said loudly in return. "I do

not care if you were to save every soul on earth from the Tribulation and Armageddon, you are still an Englishman and rudeness to a young woman is simply not done, and you know that Holmes!"

For a moment, Holmes was taken aback by my rebuke, but then he turned as we heard a clatter of a carriage stopping at our door on Baker Street. Holmes looked out and then turned to me with a smile.

"My dear friend, I am about to be redeemed, if not on my own merits then by comparison. There is one, *the one,* coming up the stairs the laces of whose shoes I am not worthy to tie up when it comes to lacking feelings and being consumed only with facts."

"You don't mean...?"

"That is exactly who I mean. My brother Mycroft has departed from his *sanctum sanctorum* and is paying a most unusual visit to his little brother, conveyed here by another one of Lestrade's conspicuously inconspicuous carriages."

From my others stories about Sherlock Holmes the reader will remember that Mycroft Holmes did not merely work for the British Government, he *was* the British Government. His title was some nondescript assistant to some non-descript Secretary, but, in his head, he held the exact memory of everything that had taken place in Westminster, or Whitehall, or in every far-flung corner of the Empire for the past thirty years. He was the *eminence grise* behind every minister or prime minister. It mattered not which party was in power. He had memorized the dossier on every Member of Parliament of every party and knew far more about them than they could afford to have set free on the streets of London. He was paid well to know everything, to advise on all significant concerns, and to say nothing.

He never left his small office in a back corner of Westminster, and that he would come to Baker Street was a unique event, portending matters that must be of the gravest concern to the Empire.

"Your brother is here," said Mrs. Hudson, opening the door, and looking wide-eyed and close to panic.

"Do show the old boy in," said Holmes, remaining in his chair and rapidly lighting up a pipe.

If I ever wondered what Sherlock Holmes might look like in ten years, I had only to observe his older brother. Mycroft Holmes was as tall as Sherlock but carried twenty-five more pounds of flesh, equal parts muscle and fat. His hair had gone snowy white, but the eyes burned with the same intensity as his brother's. The fraternal resemblance was easily guessed even before they opened their mouths and removed all doubt.

"Ah," said Holmes the younger, refusing to rise, "how nice of you to drop by Mycroft. I assume you were in the neighborhood and stopped in for a cup of tea. Let me call for one."

"Stop the nonsense, Sherlock," the older brother thundered. "You know that I would never bother to come into this silly headquarters of yours were it not on matters of extreme importance to the Government. It is a state secret and cannot be discussed here. Now fetch your coat and hat and come with me to Westminster. At once!"

Sherlock Holmes did not budge an inch. Instead, he took a slow draft on his pipe and even more slowly exhaled it.

"My dear brother, May I suggest that rather than consulting me you call on one far more qualified than I to assist you."

"Who?! And do not be deliberately obtuse." Mycroft barked in response.

"Why the tooth-fairy of course. She is the one to whom missing teeth are entrusted. Alternatively, you might check the back of your upper jaw. Missing wisdom teeth do appear there from time to time."

The older fellow's face went red with anger. "Confound you, Sherlock!" Mycroft shouted, banging his walking stick harshly on the floor. "How in the devil do you know about that? It is the most sensitive matter the Government has faced in a decade. Who told you?!"

"Why, my dear brother, you did. What possible alternative is there? A woman, whose father was the expert on The Tooth and recently murdered, shows up in my rooms, sent by Scotland Yard. An hour later you do the same thing sent by the same incompetents. All other alternative explanations are impossible, and as I have said many times…"

"Blast you! I know what you have said," Mycroft replied. He glared for a moment at his younger brother and then slowly removed his overcoat and hat, laid them on the sofa, and dropped his large body into the chair that was recently vacated by a much more attractive one.

I stood up and said, "If state secrets are about to be discussed I really must excuse myself."

"Sit down," Mycroft snarled back at me. "All you ever write about are Sherlock's successes. His failures, and they have been legion, never appear in *The Strand*. Nobody will hear anything from Sherlock's simpering Boswell unless Sherlock succeeds, so stay where you are. You might be useful for something, which is why I assume Sherlock keeps you around."

I said nothing, fearful of poking the bear in our midst. Sherlock Holmes though was not about to give up a fraternal rivalry without at least one more lick at it.

"I'm dreadfully sorry, dear brother, but I have just accepted another case. My client may be in some danger, and I must act immediately to look after her protection."

"Stop it, Sherlock! Mary Morstan is being followed to the Capital and County Bank by two armed marines. Another three will be guarding her lodgings at Mrs. Cecil Forrester's around the clock. Your client is taken care of better than you ever could."

"Why thank you for that. However, there are other clients whose concerns are pressing on me. I do not see how I can neglect them."

"You do not have any other clients. You docket is empty. Now stop the foolishness."

"You have access to every police detective, military intelligence expert, or clairvoyant in the land that your heart might desire, all courtesy of Her Majesty's Treasury. I cannot see why I should take this on."

Here Mycroft leaned forward and glared at his brother. "You *will* take it on Sherlock. You will take it on because it is dangerous, perplexing and bound to be interesting. You know that it will be anything but boring. You already know that I have no idea how to solve it or I would not be here. So you will accept it because you cannot refuse it. Now just drop the pretense and get to work."

Sherlock Holmes sat back and drew again on his pipe. I gathered that I was witnessing a ritual that had taken place many times in the past between these siblings. For a moment,

I allowed myself the delightfully wicked thought that they positively deserved each other.

"Well then Mycroft, since I am to be pressed into service without even having taken the Queen's shilling, please proceed and tell me all I need to know."

"The first thing you need to know," lectured Mycroft, "is that this is a matter of the greatest secrecy. If any word of this should get out, there will be hell to pay. It could be a disaster for the Empire."

"My dear brother," said Holmes, after yet another slow exhalation, "you know that I do not care a fig for your precious Empire. However, I have been engaged by a client who is closely connected to this matter, and you know that I would withstand torture before betraying the confidence of the young woman, or any other client for that matter."

"I suppose I do know that. Hmmm. Very well. The facts, in brief, are these — you can learn the details from Scotland Yard."

Sherlock Holmes interrupted his brother. "Scotland Yard has been informed? How many there know about this? Any others?"

"Due to its sensitivity, it has been confined to a very select few. Buckingham Palace, of course. Lestrade and two of his men. The Foreign Secretary and the Home Secretary and their private secretaries. That is all."

"Splendid," said the young brother. "That gives us three complete days to solve everything before it becomes headlines in every paper in the country. Four if we include the rest of the Empire."

"Enough sauciness, Sherlock," Mycroft muttered. "I have

enough things trying my soul today without having to put up your jibes. Now then, here is what you need to know. The Tooth was placed in an ivory box, wrapped inside a padded shipping case and put into a small but new and secure safe before leaving the temple in Kandy. It was under guard as it was taken by rail to the harbor at Trincomalee. Then it was put on a cruiser and brought by the Royal Navy all the way to the Docklands, stopping only in Cape Town for resupply. It was unloaded under guard and taken to the British Museum, and again kept under guard. When the safe was opened so that the display could be set up, it was discovered that the box was empty. The Tooth was gone."

"Ahh, a tooth-napping. And the ransom demand?" said Holmes the younger.

"Not a word."

"You have interrogated all those who had access to it? The marines who were guarding it?"

Here, out of loyalty to her Majesty's forces, I had to interject. "The Royal Marines are sterling chaps of unquestioned loyalty. It is inconceivable that they would betray such a trust."

During the years that I have known Sherlock Holmes, I have been the victim many times of what I have called The Look. In its mildest form, one of supercilious condescension, it says to me, without a word being uttered, that I am behaving like a naïve schoolboy. In mid-range, it accuses me of being a pathetic dupe. The more severe variety announces that I am revealing to all that I am no more than an imbecilic moron. What I was faced with was the middling variety delivered, however, in unison by both of the grim Brothers Holmes.

Mycroft dismissively responded, "Everyman has his price,

Watson. With a hundred pounds, you could turn one of the Queen's own Grenadiers. As to the marines guarding The Tooth, there were never less than four of them on any watch. Individually they might be suspect. However, while any one of them could have been bought off, they will never betray their fellow marine, and a collusion of that many just does not happen. They do have some principles."

Sherlock Holmes continued. "The Museum guards? They could be had for a fiver."

"They were not used. Only the marines and the monks."

"Very well, the monks then. Perhaps there is a fanatic amongst them. Have they been questioned? Surely someone in the Foreign Office could translate from Sinhala."

Here Holmes-the-elder shrugged. "It appears that the particular order of monks who guard The Tooth has taken a vow of silence, so we have not spoken to them. Demanding that they break their vow would be to them as offensive as putting the Archbishop in a whorehouse. So, no. But they are no more than a lot of dazed and doped-up fakirs who do nothing but burn incense and pray all day long and worship their deity's dentures. They would be confining their souls to hell, or whatever they have to serve the same purpose if they were to even touch the sacred relic. So we have ruled them out."

"If you have ruled out financial gain, as well as religious fervor, what then could be the motive?" asked Sherlock Holmes. "What theory have you reached?"

Mycroft Holmes sat in silence briefly and then spoke slowly. "To wreak absolute and desperate havoc upon the Empire. If the word goes out amongst the colonies that we have carelessly lost a most sacred relic of the Buddhist faith, it would be the greatest possible embarrassment to us. Utterly humiliating. But worse, there would be rioting in the streets from Banjul to Hong Kong. It would make the ruckus of 1857 or even the Boxer blow-up seem no more than a picnic by the Serpentine."

"But who on earth would want to embarrass the Queen and the British Empire?" I said and no sooner had the words left my mouth than The Look led me to regret them.

"Good Lord, Watson," said Mycroft Holmes. "I am sure that there could not be more than a five hundred million people on earth who would be of that persuasion. The Mohammedans, the Hindus, and the Buddhists would join forces overnight and start cutting our throats in the streets."

Here I felt myself on safer ground. "When I was in Afghanistan, I observed many of those faiths, and they rather did not like each other at all. If brought together, they could not agree on the time of day. How say you that they would collude against us?"

Yet again, The Look. In unison. This time, Sherlock Holmes took it upon himself to enlighten me. "My dear doctor, you are quite correct in your observation, but you cannot forget that while they do not like each other in the least, they dislike us even more. You might say 'The enemy of my enemy, and the enemy of his enemy are my friends.' There is nothing like a shared foe to unite the heathen."

I had to admit that he had a point there, and so said nothing else, but found myself worrying about what a dreadful and treacherous mess our young client had stumbled into. Neither Holmes spoke for a minute and to my relief sat and glared at each other, mercifully ignoring me.

"Very well, Mycroft," said Sherlock Holmes. "I will

devote myself to your cause and do my bit for the Empire, and my very best for my client."

"Very good," the elder brother replied. "Keep me informed about any matter as it occurs. None of your grandiose saving everything for your *deus ex machina* at the end of the play. I have neither the time nor the patience for your theatrics." With this, he stood and departed. Holmes and I sat in silence until we heard the unmarked police carriage depart.

Chapter Four
In Quest of a Solution

irst things first, Watson," said Holmes rising from his chair. He descended the stairs and opened the door to Baker Street. I heard the distinct coded set of blasts on his whistle that he used to summon his beloved Baker Street Irregulars. Through the window, I could see about half a dozen of them assemble in front of him. I watched as he chatted with them for a few minutes and then sent them scattering off toward the center of the city. He then turned, climbed back up the stairs and entered the room.

"There are three matters upon which I would value your insights, my friend," he said.

"So far today my value appears to have been worthless," I said, not a little hurt by three visitations of The Look by the Brothers Holmes.

"Oh please, Watson. There is a sporting chance that, unlike those matters you commented on earlier, you might, in fact, know something about these items.

"The first matter," he continued, ignoring whatever damaged feelings I was still nursing. "You did indeed serve in Afghanistan. As you know, during the interval after my death at Reichenbach Falls I spent some time in Tibet. Both of us have rubbed shoulders with scores of Buddhist monks, have we not?"

"Yes, I'm certain I did. I suppose you did as well."

"You suppose correctly. We have, but Mycroft has not. So did you ever come across any order of Buddhist monks that had taken a vow of silence? Or did you ever even hear of such an order?"

I paused, searching my memory. "Now that you mention it, never. They were all rather chatty and cheerful chaps. When they were done their shift in the temples, they would be on the sidewalks and in the local restaurants talking and laughing and enjoying their everlasting bowls of curried rice."

"My experience as well. Even in the most holy of temples in Tibet, they might have been quiet while on duty, but they erupted into pleasant conversation much as our English schoolboys do when let out of church. So our muffled monks are the first place for us to start our search for the missing molar."

"And the second?"

"You are a medical man, and a very learned one, I

gratefully acknowledge. Have you ever known rigor mortis to set in within a few minutes? And how can you account for that in three men, within a period of two weeks?"

"Poison of some sort. Must be."

"My conclusion as well. Yet most poisons, such as strychnine, or arsenic, or even curare from South America, while they lead to paralysis take at least an hour, and the muscles do not stiffen for nearly two. How then the immediate effect?"

I searched my memory, frustrated that it was nowhere near to matching the prodigious capacity of Sherlock Holmes. I smiled when a name and an incident popped into it. "Did I not read of some case in the past two years involving a Dr. Thomas Cream? That nasty Canadian fellow who distilled the venom of the Russell's viper. He did in a number of prostitutes who were all found with bodies as hard as cement, were they not?"

"Yes. Thank you, my friend," he said and then walked to his bookshelf. "Ah, you have confirmed my research. Here it is."

He had his scrapbook, his *Encyclopedia of Crime,* as he insisted on calling it, opened to the reports on the notorious serial killer. "Just like the villainous Dr. Cream, our murderer has used a means that, unlike a revolver, is completely silent, but unlike most poisons acts almost immediately, leaving the victim no time to call for help or to name the murderer in his dying breath. A diabolically clever killer indeed."

"Please, Holmes. Stop rubbing your hands in glee. If coming upon a fiendish killer makes your hardened heart go all pitter-pat, at least have the decency to keep your reaction hidden. Now, what was the third item?"

"These notes. What do you think of them?"

I looked at the two notes that Miss Morstan had received along with the golden statuettes. I observed to Holmes that the handwriting appeared to be either from a young hand or maybe from one that was not very experienced or educated, as the letters were uneven and jumped above and below the writing line. They were also distinctively and unusually wide and open letters. Women tend to make their letters rounder than men, but these were exaggerated, as if they were drawn rather than being written. Hard to say, since all I had to go on was the two short messages, but the tone was curiously intimate, as if the writer knew Miss Morstan. The sign used for the signature I could make nothing of.

"This sign looks like the number three pushed over on its side. Beyond that, I have no idea."

"Very good. Very good indeed Watson. The sign is, I believe, a letter in the Sinhalese alphabet." As he said this, he walked over to the bookcase and extracted a thick volume and turned the pages for several minutes.

"Ah ha. Here it is. One of the most artistically attractive and rounded ways of writing on earth. Look at this sample in the text."

යේ ධම්මා හේතුප්පභවා
තේසං හේතුං තථාගතෝ ආහ
තේසඤ්ච යෝ නිරෝධෝ
ඒවං වාදී මහාසමණෝ

"Whoever wrote this note most likely first learned to write in his native language, using its letters, not ours. Hence the wide rounding he gives cursive penmanship. And yes the message does betray some degree of acquaintance with Miss Morstan, most likely from her days in Ceylon. The first message is quite a pleasant one. The second one warns of danger. We may deduce that the writer learned of the death of Miss Morstan's father during the period of time between the first and the second. He appears to be very concerned about her. I must say, my friend, you may even find yourself facing a rival for her affections," he said giving me a mischievous smile.

"I beg your pardon, Holmes," said I. "You have no right to make such a remark. My feelings toward that woman, Miss Morstan, are honorable and nothing else."

"Oh ho," chuckled Holmes, "of course they are honorable. You are quite incapable of anything less. However, you have sat and watched as I have rudely offended countless clients and never leaped to their defense or rebuked me. I do detect something beyond the usual reaction of an English gentleman in your concern for her safety and feelings. Ah ha! Do I see just a hint of a blush, John Watson? I thought so."

He clapped his hand on my shoulder. I said nothing but could feel my face reddening in spite of my efforts to control my reaction.

"Do not let me interrupt your imaginings, my dear doctor. I have a copy on the shelf of Governor Hercules Robinson's *Days in Ceylon,* and I will read up on what he says about the Kingdom of Kandy and the Temple of the Tooth."

"Quite fine. I will take myself for a walk. It would do my constitution good."

"227 Lower Camberwell Road," said Holmes, shielding his face with the now opened volume.

"What are you talking about?"

"The address of Mrs. Cecil Forrester. You are trying to read it on Miss Morstan's card on the table without bending over. It's quite a hike from here, across the Vauxhall Bridge and past the Kennington Oval. But I am sure that in two hours you will have enough time to walk all the way, stand upon the sidewalk feeling lovelorn for as long as you need, and return in time for an outing this evening in search of the Lost Tooth."

I said nothing. I pulled the door smartly behind me. A walk along Grosvenor Street and down to the Thames would be just the thing for a summer evening. Perhaps even past the river.

Chapter Five
Where's the Curry?

I returned to Baker Street later in the afternoon. I was all prepared for Holmes to be poking fun at me again, but I was met instead with a somber look on his face.

"Is Mrs. Forrester's place well guarded? How many men were there?"

"I counted four. All in plain clothes. All strapping fellows. I would guess they were marines."

"Excellent. Those are Mycroft's men. Far better than the local bobbies. Trained to the top degree and armed to the hilt. Four of them could fight off an army and still break for tea if they had to. That's good. Our client may need them. And so may we this evening."

"Why are you saying that?" I asked, feeling alarmed by his words.

"We have two missions ahead of us this evening my friend. Please enjoy your supper quickly, and we will then have to be on our way."

I sat and ate the leg of chicken that Mrs. Hudson had prepared while Holmes brought me up-to-date on the case.

"This note arrived an hour ago from Miss Morstan."

I took the note in hand. It read as follows:

> *Mr. Holmes and Dr. Watson: This message was waiting for me when I returned to Mrs. Forrester's. As it states that I may bring friends, may I beseech you to stand for me in that role?*

It was signed: Mary Morstan. The message to which it referred read as follows:

```
Be at the stage door of the
Alhambra Theater tonight at
seven o'clock. If you are
distrustful, bring two friends.
I have news concerning your
father. We have met before. You
will recognize me. I am an old
friend.
```

"I know you well enough," I said to Holmes, "to be certain that you told her we would come."

"And I know you well enough to tell her that you, my dear friend, would be with me. Ah, there is a knock on our door, and I suspect that the captain of the Company of Irregulars is reporting."

Mrs. Hudson opened the door and in an exasperated voice announced, "One of your ruffians Mr. Holmes. Really."

In bounded a young lad whom I had met several times before. It was young Gordon Wiggins, the captain of the force. Had he had a better fortune and born to an upper-class family I am certain he would have been on his way to becoming the Lord of the Admiralty. Instead, he was destined to be confined to the streets of London.

"Yes, Captain Wigggins," said Holmes, cheerfully. "Stand forth and deliver your report. At attention now, young soldier."

The boy smiled back. "Mr. Holmes sir, we did what you told us to, sir, and we spied out the Museum looking for some fellows in orange dresses, we did sir. And sure enough, we spotted them, at least the Injin, he spotted them. He knew what to be looking for sir. They all had long coats on covering their dresses, sir, but the Injin, he saw four of them and says that they was wearing orange dresses underneath sir."

"*The Injin?*" queried Holmes. "I do not recall your having told me about him before."

"Aye. He's the new boy sir. Just off the boat from India and dark he is, sir. So we're calling him the Injin. He's real quiet like, sir, and just a skinny little fellow, but smart as a whip he is sir. Been with us now for a couple weeks, sir. Cleverest spy we got sir. And he speaks a whole lot of different tongues sir. Especially those from India sir."

"Very good, Gordon," said Holmes with a smile. "And

41

what did you learn about my odd chaps in the orange dresses?"

"Seems, sir, that there's four of them and they're doing shifts every twelve hours. Twelve on and twelve off. They enters by the back door of the Museum and they goes right down to the basement where they sits around a bunch of cases and does nothing but burn their incense. Then when their shift relief comes they gets up and goes to their rooming house, right nice one it is sir, over near Saint P's, sir. Here's the address, sir. And they goes in there and they comes out again twelve hours later and changes places and does it all again. The local fellows over there, we asked them, and they been watching them now for a week sir. Real odd blokes they said they was, sir, wearing orange dresses and all."

"Thank you, Gordon. As always you have performed above and beyond the call of duty. You will let me know when you have additional news?"

"Right sir. We left the Injin over there, sir. He said he's going to be watching the house and waiting for anyone else to show up. He's reporting to me sir as soon as he does, sir."

"Excellent. Now then here is your soldier's pay. Two for you and one for every other lad who helped. And perhaps two for this Injin chap. We wouldn't want to lose a sharp new recruit would we?"

"Right sir. Will report back tomorrow morning sir." He bounded down the stairs and out onto Baker Street, slamming the door behind him with a bang that rattled the dishes. Mrs. Hudson entered and removed the supper dishes and gave Sherlock Holmes quite the glare. He smiled back at her serenely.

"Come, Watson, the game is afoot. I have asked your

lovely young lady-friend to meet us in the middle of Leicester Square at half-past six o'clock. Between now and then we have enough time to take a cab over to Saint Paul's, see the rooming house of the monks, and learn what they are up to."

We hailed a hansom on Baker Street, and the driver hustled quickly along Marylebone Road to a pleasant residential area just north of the Saint Pancras station.

"I have no doubt, Holmes," said I, "that you have a plan in mind that will permit us to walk into a posh rooming house and demand information about their guests that is, by any decent standard of English manners, none of our business."

"That is exactly what we are going to do, doctor. So please remove your cravat and collar, leave your shirt open, take off your hat and put on this cap, and we will appear as the pinnacle of obnoxious busy-bodies who do nothing else but stick their noses into other people's business and repulsively invade their privacy."

"Aha! We are posing as members of the British Press. Splendid."

I took off my silk hat and donned the cheap, worn cap that Holmes had retrieved from a pocket in his jacket. By the time the cab had arrived at the address, we had done our best to look cheaply dressed and unkempt. We left our walking sticks and anything else that might identify us as gentlemen and asked the cabbie to wait around the corner.

Before approaching the front door, Holmes slid his body through the hedge, and I could catch glimpses of him staring intently at the lawn and garden. He returned looking puzzled and said, "There are footprints all over the paths. Some are of normal pairs of boots, and some are unshod, obviously the monks. But there is one set that is curious. There is only the print of the right foot and a deep circular indentation of about four inches in diameter and, not far away, a smaller circular indentation of only one inch."

"Captain Ahab perhaps," I said. "A wooden leg and supported by a crutch or a cane. The leg being bitten off by a great white whale."

Holmes smiled at my attempt at wit. "You are most likely correct, although there is no need to postulate a whale. Men lose legs for far more common reasons. In battle, for instance. I am sure you saw that in Afghanistan."

"Far too often, yes."

Holmes said no more but walked up to the steps and knocked repeatedly on the door.

A large Celtic-looking fellow opened it. "Jeeesus, Mary, and Joseph, you don't have to be waking the dead. Once is enough. And what is it you two blokes might be wanting? Sure as you aren't looking for decent lodging as we wouldn't be allowing the likes of you in here," he said with a look of disdain at our disheveled habits.

"Oswald Spengler's the name. *The Evening Star* of London's the paper, my good chap," said Holmes, forcing a card on the burly Irishman. "We learned from our sources that you are keeping in secret some foreigners who have come from the tropics, and they might be carrying Esmeralda fever after being in contact with the goblooks bird. This here is a doctor of medicine, and we are here to examine them and make sure they won't be spreading an epidemic amongst the good citizens of London."

Holmes began to walk into the house, but he was blocked by the large body of the housekeeper.

"Well now, isn't that a shame that those fellows just aren't going to able to meets with the likes of you. We do indeed have some very special visitors from overseas staying here. Right important chaps they are. But they're having their dinner now, so you will just have to say you tried but were not able to be seeing them."

"We must see them. If you will not permit us to do so, then we will have no choice but to report that you were afraid to do so for fear that the story of their contagious illness might become known to the public."

"And will it now? You don't say. Well now, me boys from the Fleet Street, it so happens that these gentlemen are not in secret at all. Every day they'll be walking from here to the British Museum in broad daylight. They will be, every twelve hours. So you can just wait until they do so again. But it won't be doing you any good seeing as they've all taken a vow of silence. You won't get a peep out of them. But you just wait for a few hours, and you can walk and talk all the way you wants to and see whats you gets."

"We have to file our story by six o'clock," snapped Holmes. "That will not give us enough time."

"Ah, dear me, so it won't. Well then, you'll just have to make one up like as you usually do. Here now, let me give you the first line. You can say, 'Soooo, it was a fine morning and I was out a walking along the Lethe...'"

With this, he let out a loud laugh and closed the door in our face.

"Well that was a waste of time," I said as we walked away.

45

"Not at all. Not at all," said Holmes. "A very small thing has told us much. Tell me, what did you smell coming from inside the house?"

I thought for a moment. "Nothing unusual. It smelled like supper was being served. Rather like a good Irish stew, just what you might expect to find in a rooming house kept by an Irishman."

"Exactly," said Holmes, beaming. "And when did you ever see a Buddhist monk eating Irish stew?"

"Cannot say as I ever did. They couldn't eat anything that was not drowned in curry."

"And did you smell curry wafting from the kitchen?"

"Not even a hint. You are telling me, are you Holmes, that whoever is having supper there is anything but a Buddhist monk."

"Exactly."

"So are we just going to leave them there now?"

"Of course, we are. They can do nothing but go back and forth to the Museum, and the house is being watched by Gordon's new boy, the one he calls the Injin, and who seems to be quite up to snuff for the task."

I turned and looked back at the house. From behind a lamppost, a slight brown-skinned figure wearing an oversized turban emerged and looked back at me. He raised his small hand and gave a timid wave.

Chapter Six
The Tragedy at the Alhambra

What though the spicy breezes blow soft o'er Ceylon's isle;
Though every prospect pleases, and only man is vile?

Another cab ride took us to Leicester Square. It was approaching half past six o'clock and, while there was still light in the sky on this summer evening, the dense drizzly fog lay low on the great city, rendering the entire atmosphere eerie and ghostlike. In the square, the crowds were already starting to gather for the evening theater performances. The show at the Alhambra was a popular one.

A local troupe was doing a series of hilarious sketches making fun of the German Kaiser and his sidekick, Chancellor Otto von Bismarck, and the seats were all sold out. Hopefuls were lined up thinking that they could get last minute rush seats or a place in the stands. Carriages were rattling up discharging their cargoes of shirt-fronted men and beshawled, bediamonded women.

In the middle of the square, just after half past six, we found Mary Morstan. She was outfitted in a stunning royal blue long dress, with a black silk jacket, clasped by a fine string of pearls. She was looking absolutely beautiful. I could not help but remark on how well she was bearing up under such stress.

"I confess, Doctor Watson, that I am no longer pursuing the eight-fold path to enlightenment. It has been reduced to seven. I put seven of my Buddhas into the safe box at the bank and accepted a large deposit from Sotheby's for number eight. Then I visited Regent Street, and while it may make me seem like nothing more than a shallow, materialistic girl, it does wonders for the spirits to know that I look attractive, especially when I know I am going to be meeting a handsome man in the West End of London. I smiled at her and offered her my arm, which, to my joy, she accepted with a smile. The three of us walked over to the east side of the Square and stood before the front of the Alhambra.

Suddenly a cry went up. "FIRE!! FIRE!! The theater's on fire!" We watched in shock as hundreds streamed in panic out of the front doors. I could see more exiting at the side. I feared that someone would fall and be trampled. The panic that had set in was terrifying. A moment later I heard the fire wagons clanging and the thundering hoof beats of the horses. As the last of the patrons and staff were emerging, all coughing and gasping, the brave men of the fire department were running into the burning building pulling hoses behind them. Soon they had to retreat as the flames engulfed the front of the theater. A crowd had gathered, and the bobbies kept shouting at the people to stand back. When the façade of the building cracked and fell into the street, the crowd jumped back in fear. The heat from the flames could be felt, and I knew that had anyone been trapped inside they would by now have been either burned to death or overcome by the acrid smoke and fumes. It had been no more than ten minutes since the first cry went up and the old building was already a raging inferno.

"Come. Quickly," said Holmes. "It is not yet seven o'clock. The fire is confined to the front of the building. Our appointment may still be around at the stage door."

We pushed and shoved our way through the crowds, dodged the police and fire vehicles that were approaching by way of Cranborn and Bear Streets, and worked our way south on Charing Cross Road to the back of the Alhambra. The spectators there were fewer, but the fire wagons and the firemen and the bobbies were crowded around the doors. The firemen had dragged their hoses in through the back doors and were fighting the flames from the vantage point of the still untouched stage and backstage sections of the building. I could see Holmes scanning the doors and the crowd looking for anyone who might be looking for us. I could see no one.

"Stand back! Stand back!" a shout went up. "Stretcher coming through. Stand back."

From the stage door came two firemen each carrying an end of a canvas stretcher. On it was a man's body, dressed in a tweed suit. Sherlock Holmes pushed his way through the crowd until he was walking alongside the stretcher bearers.

He reached for the arm of the man and attempted to place it on top of his body.

"Sir!" shouted one of the bearers. "Do not be touching him. He's dead already."

"Forgive me," said Holmes. "I was just trying to give him a little comfort."

"Too late for that, sir. Fumes must have got to him. He was just inside the back door but stiff as a board when we got to him. Poor bloke, almost made it out. Must have inhaled some poisonous gasses in there."

The stretcher bearers were walking toward Miss Morstan and me. Suddenly she let out a cry and covered her face with her hands. She buried her face into my chest, and I placed my hand on the back of her head and tried to comfort her. Between her sobs, I could hear her whispering, "I know him. I know him."

Sherlock Holmes led us up Charing Cross Road to a small pub, the Bear and Staff. The patrons had all vacated to watch the fire, and we were able to find a quiet table in the corner.

"I can see that you are in distress, Miss Morstan, but please, I beg you, compose yourself enough to tell me about this man. You said you knew him. Who was he?"

I wanted again to rebuke Holmes, but I recognized that he was devoted solely to stopping whoever was behind this rash of murders and protecting his distraught client from harm. I gave my handkerchief to Miss Morstan, and we waited until she had taken two or three deep breaths and looked up at Holmes.

"His name was Bartholomew Sholto. His father was Major John Sholto, my Uncle John."

"What was his connection to the project your father and the major were working on," pressed Holmes. "What did he have to do with the Tooth?"

"I don't know. I don't know," she gasped. "All I know is that he worked for the Foreign Office. He had the Ceylon Desk. He wasn't the scholar that Father and Uncle John were, but he read and spoke the ancient language. I had met him on three occasions on visits to my father. I don't know what he was doing with them. I'm sorry, but I just don't know."

To his credit, Holmes was decent and civil and even considerate in responding to her. He ordered a round of brandies for us, and we sipped them in silence. Upon finishing, he turned to Miss Morstan and said, "I am going to impose on my good friend, Dr. Watson, to see you back to your home. I'm sure he will not object, will you my good doctor?"

"Not at all. I was going to offer."

"That is very kind of you," she said. We walked out into the still drizzling evening. A street Arab offered us a large umbrella for a price that was close to banditry, but I paid him and we continued back to the Square to look for a cab.

Miss Morstan looked up into my eyes. "It really is quite a pleasant evening, and under this umbrella, the rain is not a bother. I think it would be good for me if we could just walk. It is a bit of a hike all the way across Vauxhall Bridge, would you mind, John? May I call you John? And would you mind awfully if I held on to your arm?"

The dark eyes were irresistible, and part of my heart melted inside me.

"By all means, you may, Mary." I did not admit that I knew precisely how far it was to her residence and the route to take, having walked it there and back already once earlier in the day.

I was vaguely aware of two large men walking a short distance behind us and humbly admitted to myself that this lovely young woman's safety was far better served by Mycroft's agents than by my right arm. A quick glimpse over my shoulder confirmed that they had not taken advantage of the thief bearing umbrellas and were most likely becoming soaked to the skin. But then Mycroft paid them well.

At the door of Mrs. Forrester's I bid her good night.

"Thank you, John. I do feel safe with you at my side." I mumbled some self-deprecating comment and turned to walk serenely back to Baker Street. At the first corner, I ran straight on into Mycroft's marines.

"Thank you, gentlemen," I said. "I am very grateful for your service."

"Right sir. Just doing our duty sir. Happy to oblige. We have the shift for the rest of the night and following a beautiful lady through the West End was a nice break, sir."

I gave them my umbrella and went looking for a cab.

Chapter Seven
Irish Stew

felt somewhat like a schoolboy who has been kissed by a girl for the first time in his life. As I climbed the seventeen stairs back up from Baker Street to our rooms, I stopped on several of them for a moment and remembered each part of the evening: the terror of the fire, the thrill of holding a dear young woman as she trembled, and the joy of feeling her clinging to my arm as we walked through London on a damp and foggy evening.

I entered the room only to hear the voice of Sherlock Holmes from behind his latest document. "Having trouble with the stairs, sir? The old war wound acting up? Or perhaps some other part of the constitution?"

Holmes dropped the document into his lap and smiled at me. "Why don't you pour us both a brandy. I have a long night ahead of me, and I am guessing it may be quite some time before you fall asleep."

I took the bottle off the shelf and took two snifters out of the cabinet.

"You appear to be deep into something, Holmes. Mind my asking what else you have learned since we last were together?"

"Not at all. This case is tangled and puzzling, but there is one consolation, that being that Mycroft is getting no more sleep than I am. I keep sending him notes, and he keeps sending me back files and dossiers. He must have several of his bright young slaves at work around the clock, and since he is not present, I will concede that for a government officer he is exceptionally effective and efficient.

"I sent him the address of the house we visited near Saint P and, within the hour, this very official and terribly secret document came to our door. Would you like to know who we were visiting?"

"Indeed. I have been wondering all evening who was feeding Irish stew to Buddhist monks."

"My dear chap," said Holmes. "I am most certain that your mind was entirely occupied with other much more pleasant thoughts, but nevertheless, I will satisfy your feigned curiosity."

He opened a government file and laid out a small pile of papers.

"The house is known to both the Home and Foreign Offices. The title is registered to one Daniel Parnell." Here he stopped.

"And would that be a Parnell of the great clan of the recently departed Charles Parnell?"

"Indeed, it would," said Holmes. "Daniel is a younger cousin, every bit as dedicated to Home Rule as the remarkable Charles but much more inclined to violence and radical means. So far there have been no arrests, but he has been suspected in several mysterious deaths of Royalists and anti-Parnellites. He happened to be in Madrid at the same time as that miserable forger Piggott committed suicide. He had been overheard to have made threats because of the terrible damage done by the forgeries to the reputation of Charles, and the setback it brought to the movement towards Home Rule.

"The house is leased to one Michael Murphy at a rate far below what the market is bearing for comparable properties. Mr. Murphy is also known to the nameless, faceless bureaucrats that scamper before Mycroft's whip. He is known to have been closely associated with the Irish Republican Brotherhood and the Fenians. Whitehall considers his house to be the center of Fenian activity in London."

"So then, Holmes," I asked. "Have we landed into the middle of a Fenian competition with the Buddhists to see who can give the British the boots the quickest? I'm not sure I want to be on either side of that fight, nor on either side of the Home Rule battle."

"I, on the other hand," said Holmes, "consider Home Rule to be not only inevitable but an entirely just and good cause. Mycroft and I disagree strongly on that issue and have done battle royal several times over it. I fully supported the peaceful and legal means Charles Parnell was taking before his most unfortunate early death – I even believe that he had every right to divorce the woman he had not lived with for a decade and marry Kitty O'Shea – but that is beside the point.

I have no sympathy whatsoever and find it repugnant with all my heart and soul that anyone would murder another human being to advance a political cause. If that is what we are dealing with, then we are fighting people who are no more to be respected than Jack the Ripper."

"But why would some radical Fenians want to steal The Tooth of The Buddha, of all things, Holmes? What possible good can come of that?"

"It is Mycroft's theory, and I must defer to him on this, that it is all tied to what he said earlier today about the enemy of my enemy. The loss of the Sacred Tooth will cause an uproar around the world. It will divert attention and troops from Ireland, and those troops would be sent off to the Malay States, Lahore, the Andaman Islands or any other corner of the Empire where the national people are agitating to have the Empire out. It would be an ideal opportunity to rebuild the Home Rule movement after it went off the rails with the divorce and death of Parnell."

"But where does that leave us in having to find the missing relic?" I said. "And what is the connection with that poor chap who died in the fire?"

"Ah yes. Thank you for reminding me. Mycroft sent a file on him as well. As Miss Morstan correctly informed us, Bartholomew Sholto, the son of Major Sholto, was an officer in the Foreign Office. He sat the Foreign Service Exam several years ago, had risen quickly through the ranks, and had been appointed to head the Ceylon desk because of his expertise on all aspects of the island, provided no doubt by his father, the major, and his close connection with Robert Morstan."

"It still makes no sense, Holmes. Hundreds of people knew about the Tooth and scores were involved in the negotiations, transport, and security. Why these four?"

"That, my friend, remains unknown, but we may learn a little more before daybreak. Until then I am going to keep reading and re-reading all these files until I turn into a listless, faceless, soulless bureaucrat. And I suggest that you, my dear doctor, go to bed."

I rose and would have followed his suggestion except that there was a familiar banging on the door of 221B Baker Street. I moved to descend the stairs, but Mrs. Hudson was there before me and blocking young Gordon Wiggins from entering.

"It is quite all right Mrs. Hudson. I will personally make sure that nothing is damaged and he will be gone in a few minutes."

Again, the much-tried lady gave me a glaring look and let the lad free. He bounded up the seventeen stairs in four steps and barged past me into the room.

"Mr. Holmes. Mr. Holmes, sir," that lad sputtered while catching his breath. "The Injin just reported to me, sir, an I brung his report directly to you, sir, like you asked me to sir."

"Excellent, Gordon," said Holmes. "And what did the Injin report to you."

"He said, sir, that he saw a nasty lookin' chap sir, a nasty lookin' chap with just one leg, sir. He comes and visits the house sir and then he takes a cab right all the way to Brixton, sir, an the Injin he hops on the back of the cab and seein' as he is just a wee fella no one sees him, sir, an he follows the one legged chap to Brixton an he gets off by Loughborough Road, sir, an then the Injin follows him to number 209 Cold Harbour Lane. An the Injin says it's a right frightful place sir with a very large and nasty dog sir. So, he couldn't be goin' and peekin' in the windows, sir, but he says that must be where the one-legger stays, sir, because he sees him leavin' in the mornin' sir, an goin' back to the first place and then back to Brixton again this afternoon, sir. An so he tells me this, an I'm bringin' the report to you, sir. Oh, an somethin' I forgots, sir. The Injin he says to tell you that the place smells to high heaven of curry, sir. "

"Excellent Gordon," said Holmes giving the lad a friendly clasp on the shoulder. "Now then, just wait a minute and I will give you a message that must be delivered immediately."

Sherlock Holmes sat at his writing desk and wrote a lengthy note. He folded it, wrote the address on an envelope, placed the note inside and handed it to Gordon. The boy looked at the address and his eyes went wide.

"Oh sir, please, you can't be sendin' me there, sir. That place, sir, it has marines and Welch guards, and Gondoliers, an Calvary sir, an they would shoot the likes of me sir as soon as they saw me, sir. I can't go near that place, sir."

"Ahh, yes," said Holmes. "Now just wait another minute and I can look after that." He opened the drawer of his desk, pulled out a signet stamp and stick of sealing wax. He melted a few drops on the envelope and applied the stamp. "There you go, Gordon. That will get you past anyone who stands in your way. Now off you go. And on the double."

Gordon did not look at all convinced but took the envelope and proceeded down the stairs, slowly.

Chapter Eight
Your Service Revolver

No sooner had he departed than there was another knock on the door at Baker Street. This time, Mrs. Hudson sent up a young man dressed in a page's uniform. "Sherlock Holmes and Dr. John Watson?" he inquired politely as he entered the room. I nodded and took an envelope from his hand. Holmes paid him and sent him off.

The note read:

Dr. Watson and Mr. Holmes:

Please, I beseech you,provide constant guard for Miss mary Morstan. Her life is in danger. Jonathan Small will kill her. He is very dangerous. Your lives are also at risk.

In loving concern,

"Holmes," I said. "What do you make of this?"

"Someone else," he said, "in addition to you, my dear doctor, seems to be anxious about the well-being of your Miss Morstan. I do not know who it is, but he appears to be on our side. As we need friends, I welcome the help. Now I must read and re-read whatever data I have and wait for Mycroft to respond" said Holmes I suggest again, my dear Watson, that you get to sleep as quickly as possible as we will most likely be out and about on the streets of London well before dawn."

I appreciated his thoughtful suggestion and did as he advised. As it was not yet late in the evening, it took me some time to fall asleep but eventually I drifted off.

I was awakened by Holmes firmly shaking me by the shoulder. "Come, Watson, once again the game is afoot, and it promises to be an interesting night. Please get dressed as quickly as possible."

A glance at my watch told me it was four o'clock in the morning. I splashed some water on my face and pulled on an informal set of clothes. A surprise awaited me when I entered our sitting room. I stopped and stared, for in one chair sat Mycroft Holmes, dressed as he always was as if he were on his way to have tea with the Queen, and in the other chair sat the lovely Mary Morstan, dressed in a dark blue frock and holding a black hooded cloak.

"Good morning, John," she said with a warm and beautiful smile.

"What, in heaven's name ..." I began.

"I sent for her," said Holmes. "We needed someone on short notice who could speak the Sinhala language, and she was the logical choice. And, to my delight, she has brought some valuable data with her. Would you care to tell the good doctor and my brother what you discovered?"

"Certainly, sir," she answered. "I spent the past several hours going through my father's papers and found the file that dealt with the project of The Tooth. In it were many items of correspondence but also this one page that is headed *The Cognoscenti*." She handed it first to Mycroft Holmes, who then handed it to me. On it were five names, and they read:

```
Robert Morstan
John Sholto
Thaddeus Sholto
Bartholomew Sholto
Chandraratna Widjikulaseria
```

I looked up at Holmes. "Four of these men are now dead. Who is this fourth one, Thaddeus Sholto? What is his connection?"

Mycroft replied, "He is the son of Major Sholto and the twin brother of Bartholomew. He is also with the Foreign Office but stationed in Ceylon. He works out of Government House in Colombo but was the principle colonial contact on this Tooth thing."

"Well then," said I, "at least he is not likely to end up stiff and dead if he is half the world away."

"He arrives on board a naval vessel this morning. It is due to dock at the Greenwich Pier at seven o'clock," said Mycroft brusquely. "If someone were waiting for him he would be an easy target. There would be no time to warn him before he came down the gangplank."

"Do you believe our one-legged man is out to get him as well? Is he our killer?"

"Most likely," said Holmes. "His file is on the table, but Mycroft can tell you about him briefly."

"His name is Jonathan Small. He is the most radical Fenian at-large in the Empire. His father was hung some fifteen years ago, one of the Fenian Dynamiters. Five years ago he took a spray of grapeshot in his lower leg in a skirmish between British Troops and the Irish Invincibles. He may have been invincible, but his lower leg wasn't. After it was chopped off, he escaped from the hospital in Dublin and slipped away from us. Last we heard someone reported seeing him in Ceylon and we have a report, hearsay only, that he was a paid assassin and may have murdered a few plantation owners, Englishmen of course. This is the first we've heard of his being back in Britain, but if he is and he is involved in this plot to steal The Tooth, then we have a very nasty piece of work to deal with."

"If our reports are correct," said Holmes. "Our murderer should be asleep in his bed in his house in Brixton. Lord willing, we should be able to take him, and free the Kandian monks without a shot being fired. So let us be off, the carriages are waiting. Did you bring you service revolver, Watson?"

I patted the outside pocket of my jacket.

"Good," said Holmes. "Mind you Mycroft has done you one better and brought six of his Royal Marines. You should not need your weapon, but it is always good to have it with us. And Watson, would you be so kind as to bring that package on the table? And please, do keep it upright." He pointed to a small package wrapped in canvas. I picked it up and felt heat radiating from it.

"Miss Morstan," Holmes continued. "You are ready?"

"What!" I shouted. "Holmes, really! You cannot possibly be expecting to bring a young woman into a situation as dangerous as we are facing."

Holmes shrugged. "Can you speak Sinhala? No? Neither can I."

I turned to Mycroft. "As a senior officer in her Majesty's Service, surely you cannot allow a woman to be part of a mission like this."

Mycroft shrugged. "We use them all the time. As General Booth once said, 'Some of my best men are women.'"

Mary Morstan slipped her arm through mine and leaned toward my ear. "At ease, John. My father used to take me on tiger hunts. And ... I loved them."

I shook my head in disbelief. Was I the only decent, civilized Englishman amongst us?

Chapter Nine
No Sign of the Tooth

There were two carriages waiting at the curb on Baker Street. The one in the rear was a large one and marked with military insignia. We boarded the smaller one and clattered off down Baker Street. In the pre-dawn darkness, the streets of London were deserted, and we were able to make good time running directly along Oxford Street, then down Regent Street and through Piccadilly Circus and on to the Embankment. We crossed at Blackfriar's and carried on into Brixton.

A block from our destination on Cold Harbour Lane we stopped and disembarked. Holmes gathered our little squad on the pavement. "Dr. Watson and I will make the first approach. Once you hear my signal, an owl's call, you may storm the door, disarm the guards and seize our killer. Be very careful as he is armed with some weapon that delivers poisoned darts. They are rather deadly."

"Please bring that canvas sack with you, Doctor," said Holmes. "As we walk perhaps you could untie the top of it."

I did and from within wafted the most delicious smell. "Holmes," said I. "This smells like Irish stew of all things. What in the name of all that is holy are you going to do with it?"

"Nothing more than neutralizing their first line of defense. Come now, the wind is blowing ever so gently from the north. We will approach the back garden gate with the wind behind us."

We made our way into the back lane and up to the gate. "Please remove the pot from the bag and hold it steady."

I did as Holmes directed. Within a minute, I saw a massive dog, an Irish Wolfhound, approach the gate. It gave a few soft barks but then stood still whimpering and wagging its tale.

Holmes dipped his fingers into the pot of stew and approached the gate. "Well, hello there Murphy, my big old boy. You smell some good Irish stew, don't you, old boy? They've been feeding you nothing but curried chicken for days haven't they, you old Irish fella, you. Now there, this is what you want isn't it?"

He held out his dripping fingers for the massive hound to lick. "There's a boy. You would like some more of that, wouldn't you?

"Watson, if you could slide that pot under the gate, I think that Murphy here, or whatever his name is, will ignore everything that happens for at least a few minutes."

I slid the pot forward, and the great hound eagerly began chomping away. His long hairy tail was swaying back and forth. Holmes put his hands in front of his mouth and let out an owl's call. "Come, we'll fall in behind the marines."

As we came around to the front of the house, I could hear a loud crash and the marines knocked down the door. There was a bit of yelling and shouting and by the time we were inside the soldiers were hustling several startled and not terribly effective guards out of the bedrooms. There was no sign of The Tooth and no sign of Jonathan Small.

Holmes took a dagger out from his pocket and approached one of the guards. "Sit him down," he said to the marine, who immediately forced the man onto a chair. Holmes placed his dagger against the man's left nostril and spoke quietly. "Where is The Tooth? If you do not tell me, I will do damage to you. Where is it?"

The fellow, who I had to admit, had more guts than brains, spat in the face of Sherlock Holmes. "I'm a citizen of the bloody Empire, and I don't have to tell you anything, and you cannot lay a hand on me." Holmes looked at the marines who in unison looked up at the ceiling and began to whistle. Holmes drove the dagger two inches into the poor chap's leg. He let out a shriek of pain followed by a stream of curses.

"A matching pair is much more stylish, don't you think my good man?" said Holmes quietly to the writhing fellow. "Would you like to feel this in your other leg?"

"Small has it! He took it with him. He has it."

"Where has he gone?"

"I don't know."

"Tut, tut," said Holmes as he lifted the dagger in the air.

"No. Honest sir. In the Virgin's name. I don't know."

"Very well," said Holmes, turning to the rest of us. "The monks are most likely in the cellar."

Two of the marines made their way down the steps. Holmes, Mary Morstan and I followed. The big fellows had come prepared and using a large jemmy broke the door open. There was limited light, and I could hear voices speaking in a strange tongue. Mary Morstan pushed her way past me and spoke some words to the inmates of the room. Four men dressed in orange monk's robes, with shaved heads, came forward. Mary continued to speak to them, and they answered back to her.

She then turned to Holmes and I and said, "They are all safe and unharmed. They are distressed about The Tooth. They took a very sacred vow to protect it, but they were overpowered and taken captive."

"Please assure them that The Tooth will soon be back in their hands," said Holmes. "And ask them if they know what happened to the man with one leg."

She spoke to them. One of them replied to her. "He says that they know the man you refer to. They saw him when they were taken and imprisoned. They hear him arrive and leave every day, and can tell it is him by the sound of his cane and wooden leg. He departed from this house just over an hour ago."

"That is not good news," said Holmes. "Come, he is on his way to Greenwich. We have to get there before he strikes his next victim."

Holmes, Mary and I hurried from the house with two of the marines. The rest were left to tend to the prisoners and the monks. Holmes opened the door of the small carriage and pulled his brother by his coat sleeve out from within. I was quite sure that Her Majesty's senior civil servant was not accustomed to such treatment, at least, not since he had escaped the urgency inflicted upon him by his younger brother when both were still children.

The four of us and our marines climbed into the large military carriage, and the driver set off at breakneck speed through the streets that led out of Brixton. Then the horses were sent galloping along Rochester Way in the direction of the Naval Yard at Greenwich. It was well over five miles to the pier, and we were fortunate that the streets had not yet become crowded with the early morning hurly-burly of London.

We arrived at the Naval Yard as the morning light was breaking. I glanced at my watch and saw that it was approaching seven o'clock. Our troop made our way quickly out onto the Greenwich Pier where the naval vessel carrying Thaddeus Sholto was pulling into the berth.

"Holmes," said I. "Look. Out there by the edge of the pier."

In the glimmering light, I could discern two figures, both standing at the spot on the pier where the ship's gangplank would be lowered.

"Does one of them have a wooden leg?"

Holmes pulled his spyglass from his inner pocket and as we hastened along the pier put it to his eye.

"Yes. That's him. Marines, take those men up there on the pier. Beware;   the chap with the wooden leg is armed."

The marines broke into a run and closed the distance between us and our target. One of them shouted, "Jonathan

Small! Your hands in the air. Do not attempt to resist or you will be fired upon!"

The two men saw them coming, stood still for a moment and then darted to the far side of the long narrow pier and disappeared over the edge. I heard an engine start up and saw a small, narrow launch pull away from the pier's edge and into the open water of the Thames. Once it was away from the shore, it turned right and sped downstream.

"Where can they go?" I shouted at Holmes. He turned and looked at Mycroft, whose eyes were closed. I recognized the fraternal look of deep concentration on his face. "I read the arrivals and departure schedule looking for this one. Yes. The *Spirit of Derry* departed Canary Wharf just minutes ago. It should be about a quarter-mile farther down the river from us by now. It's on its way to Dublin. That would be his logical escape route would it not, Sherlock?"

"Precisely," replied Holmes. "But how can we get to him? Can you have men waiting in Dublin? But he could get off at anyone of a dozen places before that."

"Begging your pardon, sir," said the youngest of the marines, a massive strapping fellow who looked as if he would be as dangerous in a scrum as on the battlefield. He stepped up to the Brothers Holmes and gave a salute. "Begging your pardon, but sir we are marines and we do know how to pilot a boat, sir. And if it would not be too much against regulations sir, I happen to see a couple of fine fast launches tied up right beside us sir. If one of them were to be borrowed for a bit by Her Majesty, I would think the owner wouldn't mind too much, sir."

"Excellent," said Mycroft Holmes. "Very good indeed. Boys, cast off and full steam ahead."

We lowered ourselves into some good citizen's new launch. I marveled at how Mycroft could keep his walking stick in hand, his silk hat on his head and his cravat perfectly in place while lowering his heavy frame off of a pier.

Within five minutes the marines had the boat fired up and under way. We pulled away from the pier and opened the throttle and began to fly over the water. Once out in the current, there was a bit of a chop from the morning breeze, and we bounced and rose and dived over the waves. The damp wind struck against our skin and Mary clasped my arm tightly and buried her face into my shoulder to avoid the spray. I made a note in my mind to add this to my list of adventurous outings for a future date.

The marines stoked the engine. Sherlock Holmes leaned over the bow, peering through his spyglass. Mycroft Holmes sat with his back to the wind, his hat in his lap, and otherwise motionless — a veritable Buddha with a silk hat.

"I have spotted them," said Holmes. "They have pulled alongside that coaster. Yes, I can see a rope ladder being lowered. We should be upon them in a few minutes."

Some five minutes later our launch pulled up beside the coaster. "Customs inspection," shouted Holmes.

"Be gone with you," came a voice from the deck. "We're off to Ireland. It's still part of your bloody Empire. There's no customs inspections that can touch us."

"Allow us to board, sir," shouted Holmes, "or your vessel will be impounded."

I do not speak Gaelic, otherwise I am sure I would have understood some colorful curses directed our way. A rope ladder was tossed down, and one of the marines scampered up. The rest of us followed.

Once on the deck, Mycroft produced a badge and flashed it in front of the captain of the coaster. "On Her Majesty's Service, sir. These are Royal Marines. Now stand where you are as we search your vessel. Do not attempt to hinder us or you will be arrested."

Again, I heard some words in Gaelic, but the captain and his men stood aside and remained in the stern of the boat while we spread out. Under the salt-caked smoke stack, we worked our way past crates of Tyne coal, road rails, pig-iron, firewood, ironware and trays made of cheap tin destined to be sold at exploitive prices to the housewives of Dublin.

"He could be hiding in any one of these," I said. "We will need more help to search."

"I do not think that will be necessary," said Mary. "Mr. Small is not hiding."

She gestured toward the open section of the deck at the bow. There stood a one-legged man leaning on a cane with his right hand, and holding his left hand out over the railing.

Chapter Ten
On the Thames

We walked toward him. The marines had their pistols drawn and pointed. He continued to hold his hand over the railing, and when we were within five yards of him, he opened his fist, exposing a small box, such as one might use to hold a diamond ring.

"Come forward slowly," said Sherlock Holmes. "Hand over the box and surrender. If you do not, you will be shot."

Jonathan Small let out a quiet evil laugh. "And will I be? You don't say. Well now I have myself another idea, I do. This here, as for sure you know, is the third molar of old Buddha. And either it can go drown itself in the Thames, or you can let me pass. And while you would be at it, you will let me get back in my boat and take your boat too. So, what do you say, Sherlock Holmes, do you want your Empire to blow up on you or will you be a good cowardly Englishman and do what I says?"

With this, he gave the jewelry box a small toss into the air and caught it again. He opened it and swept his hand forward and back out again over the railing, giving a glimpse of a small gleaming white object. I heard Mycroft Holmes gasp in horror behind me. "Let him pass," he gasped. "Let him pass. The cost is too high."

Sherlock Holmes looked in anger at his brother but slowly moved aside, as did the marines. I began to do the same when I felt a movement inside the pocket of my jacket. I looked in shock as Mary lifted my service revolver, cocked it and walked to within six feet of Jonathan Small.

"*On ne passé pas.* My name is Mary Morstan. You killed my father."

"Morstan's little mongrel has more courage than the officers of the Empire, does she?" shouted Small. "Well then, how about you prepares to die?" He raised his cane about his head as he shouted.

"The cane!" shouted Holmes. "It's poisoned!"

Small was not fast enough. Mary lowered the revolver a fraction and fired. A gush of blood and bone fragment exploded from Small's right knee. He collapsed on the deck.

He let out a stream of curses and looked up at us. "Your bloody British Empire can go to hell!" He hurled the box bearing the Sacred Tooth over the side and into the depths of the River Thames. One of the marines quickly jumped forward and put his foot firmly on Small's wrist, and yanked the cane from his grasp.

Mycroft Holmes raised his hands to either side of his head and fell back against one of the stack of crates. "Oh no. Dear God. Oh no."

Sherlock Holmes looked at Mary with a look that spoke the words of anger and condemnation.

Mary turned and looked at one Holmes brother and then the other.

"At ease, gentleman," she said merrily. "It was a fake. The true Tooth has never left the Temple in Kandy."

An hour later the four of us gathered for an English breakfast at the old Cutty Sark Tavern and looked out over the Thames, the watery resting place of the tooth that was not The Tooth.

"Really quite brave of you, my dear," said Holmes to Mary. "And quite an accurate shot. Where, may I ask, did you acquire such skills?"

"My father took me on several tiger hunts. A one-legged man with a cane is nowhere near as terrifying as an approaching Bengal Tiger. Father used to say that if you were afraid, your only shot was going to miss then you had better get closer until you were sure it couldn't."

"I suppose that is good advice for hunting," said Mycroft Holmes. "I wouldn't know. However, Miss Morstan, I do believe that you owe us some sort of explanation. The government of Great Britain, the entire civil service, and even Buckingham Palace have been under the belief that the authentic Tooth of the Buddha, the Tooth that has been on display for a millennium in Kandy, had been delivered to London and was to be the centerpiece of the magnificent exhibit at the British Museum, beginning in four days from today. Your information is rather startling."

"It *is* the tooth that has been displayed and venerated by the faithful," Mary replied. "But it is not the true Tooth of the Buddha. That one is kept in a vault in the depths of the Temple. The one that is displayed is only a polished ivory copy. They would never display the real one. Not only is it far too sacred and valuable to risk its being stolen, it is brown and mottled and not very attractive, as you would expect a fifteen-hundred-year-old molar to be.

"My father and his colleagues who handled all the negotiations for the loan of the tooth knew this of course. Father had the honor of seeing and touching the real one many years ago. But he and Uncle John, and the Sholto boys all knew that there would be no exhibit worth anything if the authenticity of the relic were known to be false. Now Father and the major were true and loyal soldiers of the Empire, but you must remember that they became Asian scholars, very attracted to the teaching of the Buddha, and by anyone's judgment, more than a little odd. They decided among themselves that they would just keep their knowledge to themselves and not rain on the parade of the Empire."

"Ah yes," said Sherlock Holmes. "The Fenians devised a very elaborate attempt to wreak havoc on the Empire. Then that whole plot would have been for naught as it would be revealed that the stolen tooth was only a replica. Mr. Small and his gang would have plotted for over a year only to have their dreams of uprisings from Hong Kong to Haifa vanish. That is why he sought to remove the five people who knew the truth."

"Hmm, yes indeed," added Mycroft. "Of course, the truth would eventually come out but not before anger had swept the world. I gather that Small learned of the planned exhibit and hatched his plot while in Ceylon. I have received a note saying that the phony monks were four Fenians who managed to overpower the real chaps and then impersonate them, giving them the opportunity to purloin the tooth. All very diabolically worked out, and it would have all been for nothing.

"Permit me to ask, Miss Morstan," continued Mycroft. "When and how did you become aware of this information?"

Mary looked straight back at him and replied, "Yesterday afternoon, as I read through Father's files. There were some confusing notes that suggested the truth, but I could not be sure until I saw the tooth itself as Small waved it in front of us. When I saw that it was gleaming white, I knew that it could not be the authentic relic."

"Hmm, very well then," muttered Mycroft. "If you will excuse me I have to go and rescue the British Museum and the Foreign Office from what is sure to be a very angry British public once they learn that they have been misled for six months and have bought tickets to see a scrap of ivory. And Sherlock you will have to come with me and help Scotland Yard discern what to do with Jonathan Small and his gang."

Sherlock and Mycroft Holmes rose and walked toward the door. Well before they arrived at the exit of the Cutty Sark I saw a slight young lad in a turban step inside, waive his small brown hand at me and then disappear back outside.

"The Injin has been quite persistent, has he not?" I said to Mary once we were alone. "Above and beyond the call of duty for just another one of the Baker Street Irregulars, especially for a new boy. Quite the young lad."

"Yes. Put himself in some danger as well no doubt. If you ever catch up with him do let him know that I am most grateful and would love to get to know him."

"Of course, my dear," I replied and then changed the

subject to one that was giving me some distress.

"I simply have to ask you something," I said, in as kindly but serious voice as I could muster.

Mary smiled and nodded. "Ask anything, John."

"My dear, you suspected that the tooth that had arrived in London was not the authentic one. You knew the same thing your father and the major did about the real one's being kept in the vault and never taken out. Why did you not say something earlier after you knew that the only men who knew the truth were the ones that had been murdered?"

Mary said nothing and then took a slow sip of her tea.

"I fear that if I give a truthful answer, you will run away in horror and never want to marry me."

Had my intentions been that obvious? Oh dear. Nevertheless, I pressed on. "Then it is surely best that I know now before I ask you to marry me, rather than finding out afterward."

For several seconds, she gazed directly at me with her intense dark eyes.

"Revenge."

I waited to hear more, and on hearing nothing, said, "Revenge?"

"Yes, darling. Jonathan Small took the life of my father, my uncle, and two fine young men. I knew that the evidence against him for any of the murders would be weak and circumstantial and that he would most likely walk. There could not be much more than a petty fine for stealing a fake tooth worth no more than a few pounds. So, I took it upon myself to make sure that even if he lived, he would suffer for the rest of his life for what he did. If he does not swing from the gallows, then he will need two wooden legs until he dies and has to answer before God.

"So, John, that is why I shot him. If you want you can get up and walk away, and I shall only ever be thankful for your warm and caring friendship."

It took me less than a second to respond. "There is a pleasant chapel over at the Naval Yard. They probably have a priest on duty. Do you suppose he would marry us now if we asked him nicely?"

"He might, but I fancied something a little splashier than a hasty boring chapel wedding. I would look rather fetching in white, don't you think, dear?"

Chapter Eleven
Injin

I am not at all sure what Mycroft Holmes did within the government of Great Britain, or within the labyrinthine offices of the British Museum, but within twenty-four hours a sea-change came over London. Posters that for months had beckoned the citizens to "Come and View the Wisdom Tooth of The Buddha" suddenly disappeared and were replaced with ones enticing us all to "Share the Experience of The Tooth." In just the same way as the faithful in Ceylon sat before the display of the tooth, breathed the fragrant incense, were enchanted by the hypnotic *hevisi* sounds of drums and strange woodwind instruments, now Londoners, those hard-working families who would never have the opportunity to visit India and enjoy the exotic life under the Raj, could have that same experience in the intricately crafted display rooms, faithful to the smallest detail to the temples of the East.

The posters featured gorgeous young Ceylonese women in saris that exposed their mid-section, and rather more cleavage than any mother in Colombo would permit her daughter to flaunt. The pictures of the young men, all athletic and slender, were even more daring and had them all clad in sarongs with their torsos entirely bare.

The word "exotic" was used over and over again.

The Museum raided their vaults and other public or private holdings to bring out anything that came from the sub-continent. A gilded carriage, studded with gems that had belonged to some Maharajah was borrowed from some Duke. Select diamonds and rubies were borrowed from the Crown Jewels, and since they had been stolen fair and square from India, it was only decent that they should be put on display.

Overnight the Museum restaurant changed its menu and began offering several different varieties of curry with every known meat and vegetable that could be found in the summer in London. The spice-laden dishes ranged from the utterly and typically English bland to ones which would provide the patron with a near-death experience.

Upon arriving at the Museum, visitors were given the opportunity, for a small sum, of changing into a lovely, if daring, sari or a sarong. On young Britons, these looked almost attractive if you could get over the sickly pale skin. On older patrons, suffering from the effects of decades of over-eating and the ravages of gravity, they were embarrassing. But that did not stop them being enthusiastically attired and the wearers' pretending to be exotic.

In the room that held the tooth that was not The Tooth,

all lights had been extinguished except for several score of candles that lit up the glass box with the pagoda roof in which the tooth was displayed, sitting serenely on a black velvet cloth. Visitors were required to remove their shoes before coming close and warned that it was a serious travesty to point their feet at the sacred relic. The good British public obeyed reverently.

About forty young people, whose only qualification for the role was their dark skin, were quickly recruited and dressed in sarongs and saris and served as guides. They greeted all visitors with a small bow, their hands held under their chins as if in prayer, and a distinct "ayubowan" that the visitor was encouraged to return.

It was rumored that some of the racier young members of England's nobility were going to host "Tooth Parties" on their estates where guests would parade around for the weekend in saris and sarongs. Overall everything that could be thought of that would heat the blood of the English people was laid on with the predictable result that no one bothered to notice that the real tooth was five thousand miles away.

On the day of the opening of the great exhibit, I rose early and spent a little more time shaving than usual, removing all non-essential facial hair from my face.

Holmes, Mary and I were given special passes to the Museum, courtesy of Mycroft. We gawked in wonder at the displays of jewels, gold, artifacts, ancient maps, models of temples and the like. The young guides recited the story of the Tooth of the Buddha and how it had been brought by the Princess Hemamali to Kandy over one thousand five hundred years ago.

We entered the room where the tooth was on display, not wanting to miss out on The Experience of The Tooth, even if we had already had enough of an experience of the tooth to last a lifetime. We stood at the back, behind several rows of worshipful Buddhists-for-a-day.

I gave a nudge to Holmes and pointed to a small person standing near the far wall. Although the room was dark, it appeared to be the same young fellow, the Injin, who I had seen a couple of days ago. Holmes nodded and quietly walked toward him, with Mary and me following behind. When the three of us were standing behind him, Holmes leaned forward and whispered, "Good morning, Injin."

Without moving, his eyes on the display of the tooth, the young lad replied, "Good morning sir."

"Thank you for the excellent work you did for us."

"Happy to help sir. It's my job as one of your Irregulars, sir."

Sherlock Holmes said nothing for the next minute, then he leaned forward again and whispered, "Good morning, Miss Anne Morstan."

Injin did not respond. I heard Mary gasp and felt her hand clamp like a vice on my arm. Then the three of us watched as a small pair of hands lifted the turban up and one by one removed combs that were holding a mass of black hair on top of the head. With a shake, the hair tumbled down until it was covering the shoulders. Injin turned to Holmes and said, "Good morning, Mr. Sherlock Holmes," and then turned toward me and said, "Good morning, Doctor Watson."

I was looking at an exquisitely beautiful face of a dark-skinned young woman in her mid-teens. Except for the color of her skin and hair, the shape and contour of her features and her dark eyes were almost identical to Mary's.

Finally, she looked at Mary and said, "Good morning, sister."

I felt Mary's two hands on my arm and holding me very tightly. She said nothing. Her eyes and indeed her mouth were open in shock and disbelief.

Holmes intervened and stretched his long arms out around several sets of shoulders. "Enough of gawking at a fake tooth. The Museum restaurant is serving some excellent curry, and I think eating some Indian for lunch would be a capital idea." With this, he steered us toward the door.

By the time we arrived at our table, the young person who was formerly known as Injin, now Miss Anne, had removed her street boy's jacket, revealing a spotless white dress shirt, such as might be worn to one of our finer public schools. She sat down beside Holmes and across from Mary and me. The girl was obviously very tense and embarrassed and avoided looking at Mary. To relieve the tension I asked Holmes, "Really Holmes. This is amazing. How in the world did you know who this young person was?"

Holmes smiled at me and then warmly at Miss Anne. "I would like to be able to say that it was a simple matter of deduction. The notes that accompanied the gold Buddhas were in a feminine hand and conveyed a strong sense of familial concern and affection. The only person who could possibly meet those criteria would be a sister. That is what I would like to be able to say, but I cannot. The truth is that Gordon snitched." The three of us chuckled in nervous laughter. Mary continued to stare at Miss Anne, and I detected tears forming in her eyes and creeping down her fair face.

"Anything else Gordon said," continued Holmes, "is subject to skeptical review, so, if you are able to, Miss Anne Morstan, we are depending on you to tell us how it is that you have ended up sitting here with us in the British Museum."

Miss Anne said nothing and continued to stare at the space where a bowl of curried lamb would soon be sitting. Finally, she looked up and began her story in an uncertain voice.

"My father …I mean our father," she said, looking at Mary, "was a wonderful loving man, a very successful businessman, and a great scholar. But … but even I could see since the time I began school that he was what the boys in the Irregulars would call a chap who had gone a long way down queer street."

Here Mary laughed spontaneously. "Oh that he was. That he was. Lovable, brilliant, but certainly a very odd duck." She smiled warmly at her newly discovered sister.

"When my mother died giving birth to me, Father was devastated, and it completely unsettled him. He said that he was so heartbroken that he could not continue to live in Ceylon, and that having to look upon me every day — it is said that I look very much like my mother — would be too much for him to bear, so he told everyone that I had died as well. He placed me in a children's home in the care of the church, fully expecting me to be adopted by a loving Ceylonese family."

"You do look like Mother," said Mary. "It is as if I were looking now at the woman my mother would have been in her teens." Again, the tears began to flow, and I handed her my handkerchief.

"After five years," Miss Anne said, "no one had adopted me. The Ceylonese families, all of them, the Tamils, the Sinhalese, and even the Burghers who wished to adopt a child all preferred those whose skin was fairer than mine. There were many Anglo-Indian children to choose from and so I was not taken. Father used to say that we millions of Anglo-Indians were an everlasting biological monument to the adultery of the British Raj.

"When I turned five and was still living in the children's home, Father accepted that I was not going to be taken by any other family and he assumed his role as my father. But having told everyone, including his family, that I had died, he could not face the censure he would experience if he admitted that he had deceived everyone. So he continued to be a father to me in Kandy and to you in London," she said looking up at Mary.

Mary gave a shrug of her shoulders and said, "As we have said, he truly was a bit of a strange bird."

"So Father enrolled me at Hillwood College, an excellent and caring place, the sister school to Trinity College for Boys, where he had taught for so many years. Twice a year he came back to Ceylon to visit me. While I was in classes, he would do research at the Temple. Sometimes I would wait for him there after classes finished for the day and I became very familiar with the Temple and the relic of the Sacred Tooth. On weekends and holidays, we would take trips up to the tea gardens in Nuwara Eliya, or to the beaches, and sometimes to the hill country in the north of India. He told me stories of taking my sister on tiger hunts but said that he was too old for any more of them.

"I had done very well in school, especially in my maths. Father had told me that Mother had been a qualified accountant, so I learned bookkeeping and accounting to be like her. Even though I am still quite young, Father put me in charge of looking after his banking and business interests. That is how I came to be the agent for the trust that came to you," she said looking at Mary, "when you turned twenty-five.

"On his last visit this past spring he was quite excited about his role in the exhibit of The Tooth in London. He said that he would not be able to come back to Ceylon for at least a year. I was very upset with this, perhaps a bit angry, and perhaps a bit jealous that my sister would have my father all to herself. He was eighty-one years old on his last birthday, and I was terribly afraid that he would die before I ever got to see him again. I begged him to take me with him but he refused, so I decided that I would find my own way to London and I came here."

"How in heaven's name did you do that?" I asked. "Were you a stowaway?"

"Oh no," she answered. "I simply bribed one of the Royal Marines who was finished his posting. I paid him to say that I was his child and he took me on board the ship with him. That way I could bring my clothes and belongings and the set of golden Buddhas that I had to send to my sister. It was not difficult. There were several other dark-skinned children on board. No one asked any questions."

"How could you have found the Irregulars," I asked. "What would have brought you into contact with our beloved street urchins?"

"I had read all about Sherlock Holmes and his Company of Baker Street Irregulars in the stories in *The Strand,* and it seemed like such a splendid adventure. When I arrived here, I found a safe storage place for my property and then came right to Baker Street and asked Gordon if I could be an Irregular. I will have to behave like a lady for the rest of my life. This was my only chance to live a life I never would again. It truly was rather fun.

"I had planned to visit my father very soon, but then I had read the news of his death. I was very distressed, but I was also frightened. When I read that his body was found to be stiff already, I knew who had killed him. School girls in Ceylon had been warned about Mr. Jonathan Small. Several plantation owners had recently died, and their bodies had been found in the same condition. Kandy is a small place and rumors are plentiful. Stories of a one-legged man who murdered people by poisoning them with venom from vipers were well-known. I was terrified thinking that he had come to London. I was worried not for myself because I knew he would never know about me, but he would know about you, my sister."

"And so," said Holmes, "you told her to come to me, and you sent warnings, and sent information back to us through Gordon."

"Yes, sir. I did."

"All very well done, my dear," Holmes continued. "I do have one last question that I have not been able to discover the answer to."

"Sir?"

'Your notes were signed not with your name but with a letter of the Sinhalese alphabet. I have tried to discern the meaning but have not been able to deduce anything. Pray tell, why that sign?"

The young woman looked rather sheepish for a short moment and then smiled at Sherlock Holmes. "When I was just beginning school my father used to tell me stories about the legends of Ceylon and especially about Princess Hemamali, the beautiful and brave princess who smuggled the Sacred Tooth to Kandy. I loved to imagine that I was the

Princess of the Tooth and so I began to sign my name with just that letter. My father began to call me Hemamali, and he kept doing so until the last time we were together."

"But that letter is not in any of the words that are used for The Tooth of the Princess," said Holmes.

Here Miss Anne giggled. "No, but look." She took a pencil from her pocket and drew her sign on a the back of the menu.

"Can't you see?" She asked us. "It looks like a tooth. Like the third molar of the Buddha, his wisdom tooth, the one that for over one thousand years has been in the Temple in Kandy."

We all shook our heads bewildered by our inability to see what to a child had been so obvious.

"Ah, yes," said Holmes. "I see that I have been helped in my mission by the Tooth Princess. Splendid."

"In truth, sir," the young woman replied. "My father used to call me the Tooth Fairy. So I guess that is who assisted you."

"My dear girl," I said, "you are a wonder. And you have my utmost admiration. But you must permit me to ask just one more question."

"Sir?"

"Why did you not just come directly to your sister? Why hide from her?"

She dropped her eyes to the floor, looked at Mary and quietly replied, "I was afraid. I knew that you were beautiful and blonde and accomplished, and I was afraid that you would not want a darker-skinned younger sister intruding into your life."

Mary stared for a full minute at Miss Anne. No one spoke. Then Mary said, "I welcome the intrusion. You have just helped me solve an enormous problem."

Miss Anne said nothing for a moment, seeming too fearful to ask. Finally, in a quiet voice, she said, "What was that?"

"It is a problem that I will only have once in my lifetime, and you are the solution to it. I am in need of a maid-of-honor, and who better than my beautiful little sister to stand with me at my wedding."

Did you enjoy this story? Are there ways it could have been improved? Please help the author and future readers of New Sherlock Holmes Mysteries by posting a review on the site from which you purchased this book. Thanks, and happy sleuthing and deducing.

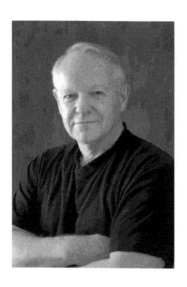

About The Author

In May of 2014 the Sherlock Holmes Society of Canada —
better known as The Bootmakers — announced a contest for a
new Sherlock Holmes story. Although he had no experience
writing fiction, the author submitted a short Sherlock Holmes
mystery and was blessed to be declared one of the winners.
Thus inspired, he has continued to write new Sherlock Holmes
Mysteries since and is on a mission to write a new story as a
tribute to each of the sixty stories in the original Canon. He
currently writes from Toronto, the Okanagan, and Manhattan.
Several readers of New Sherlock Holmes Mysteries have
kindly sent him suggestions for future stories. You are
welcome to do likewise at craigstephencopland@gmail.com.

More Historical Mysteries

by Craig Stephen Copland
www.SherlockHolmesMystery.com

 ***Studying Scarlet.*** Starlet O'Halloran, a fabulous mature woman, who reminds the reader of Scarlet O'Hara (but who, for copyright reasons cannot actually be her) has arrived in London looking for her long-lost husband, Brett (who resembles Rhett Butler, but who, for copyright reasons, cannot actually be him). She enlists the help of Sherlock Holmes. This is an unauthorized parody, inspired by Arthur Conan Doyle's *A Study in Scarlet* and Margaret Mitchell's *Gone with the Wind.*

 ***The Sign of the Third.*** Fifteen hundred years ago the courageous Princess Hemamali smuggled the sacred tooth of the Buddha into Ceylon. Now, for the first time, it is being brought to London to be part of a magnificent exhibit at the British Museum. But what if something were to happen to it? It would be a disaster for the British Empire. Sherlock Holmes, Dr. Watson, and even Mycroft Holmes are called upon to prevent such a crisis. This novella is inspired by the Sherlock Holmes mystery, *The Sign of the Four.*

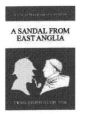 ***A Sandal from East Anglia.*** Archeological excavations at an old abbey unearth an ancient document that has the potential to change the course of the British Empire and all of Christendom. Holmes encounters some evil young men and a strikingly beautiful young Sister, with a curious double life. The mystery is inspired by the original Sherlock Holmes story, *A Scandal in Bohemia.*

The Bald-Headed Trust. Watson insists on taking Sherlock Holmes on a short vacation to the seaside in Plymouth. No sooner has Holmes arrived than he is needed to solve a double murder and prevent a massive fraud diabolically designed by the evil Professor himself. Who knew that a family of devout conservative churchgoers could come to the aid of Sherlock Holmes and bring enormous grief to evil doers? The story is inspired by *The Red-Headed League.*

A Case of Identity Theft. It is the fall of 1888 and Jack the Ripper is terrorizing London. A young married couple is found, minus their heads. Sherlock Holmes, Dr. Watson, the couple's mothers, and Mycroft must join forces to find the murderer before he kills again and makes off with half a million pounds. The novella is a tribute to A Case of Identity. It will appeal both to devoted fans of Sherlock Holmes, as well as to those who love the great game of rugby.

The Hudson Valley Mystery. A young man in New York went mad and murdered his father. His mother believes he is innocent and knows he is not crazy. She appeals to Sherlock Holmes and, together with Dr. and Mrs. Watson, he crosses the Atlantic to help this client in need. This new storymystery was inspired by *The Boscombe Valley Mystery.*

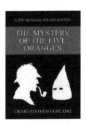

The Mystery of the Five Oranges. A desperate father enters 221B Baker Street. His daughter has been kidnapped and spirited off the North America. The evil network who have taken her has spies everywhere. There is only one hope – Sherlock Holmes. Sherlockians will enjoy this new adventure, inspired by The Five Orange Pips and Anne of Green Gables.

The Man Who Was Twisted But Hip. France is torn apart by The Dreyfus Affair. Westminster needs Sherlock Holmes so that the evil tide of anti-Semitism that has engulfed France will not spread. Sherlock and Watson go to Paris to solve the mystery and thwart Moriarty. This new mystery is inspired by, *The Man with the Twisted Lip,* as well as by *The Hunchback of Notre Dame.*

The Adventure of the Blue Belt Buckle. A young street urchin discovers a man's belt and buckle under a bush in Hyde Park. A body is found in a hotel room in Mayfair. Scotland Yard seeks the help of Sherlock Holmes in solving the murder. The Queen's Jubilee could be ruined. Sherlock Holmes, Dr. Watson, Scotland Yard, and Her Majesty all team up to prevent a crime of unspeakable dimensions. A new mystery inspired by *The Blue Carbuncle.*

The Adventure of the Spectred Bat. A beautiful young woman, just weeks away from giving birth, arrives at Baker Street in the middle of the night. Her sister was attacked by a bat and died, and now it is attacking her. A vampire? The story is a tribute to *The Adventure of the Speckled Band* and like the original, leaves the mind wondering and the heart racing.

The Adventure of the Engineer's Mom. A brilliant young Cambridge University engineer is carrying out secret research for the Admiralty. It will lead to the building of the world's most powerful battleship, The Dreadnaught. His adventuress mother is kidnapped, and he seeks the help of Sherlock Holmes. This new mystery is a tribute to *The Engineer's Thumb.*

The Adventure of the Notable Bachelorette. A snobbish nobleman enters 221B Baker Street demanding the help in finding his much younger wife – a beautiful and spirited American from the West. Three days later the wife is accused of a vile crime. Now she comes to Sherlock Holmes seeking to prove her innocence. This new mystery was inspired *The Adventure of the Noble Bachelor*.

The Adventure of the Beryl Anarchists. A deeply distressed banker enters 221B Baker St. His safe has been robbed, and he is certain that his motorcycle-riding sons have betrayed him. Highly incriminating and embarrassing records of the financial and personal affairs of England's nobility are now in the hands of blackmailers. Then a young girl is murdered. A tribute to *The Adventure of the Beryl Coronet*.

The Adventure of the Coiffured Bitches. A beautiful young woman will soon inherit a lot of money. She disappears. Another young woman finds out far too much and, in desperation seeks help. Sherlock Holmes, Dr. Watson and Miss Violet Hunter must solve the mystery of the coiffured bitches, and avoid the massive mastiff that could tear their throats. A tribute to *The Adventure of the Copper Beeches*.

The Silver Horse, Braised. The greatest horse race of the century, will take place at Epsom Downs. Millions have been bet. Owners, jockeys, grooms, and gamblers from across England and America arrive. Jockeys and horses are killed. Holmes fails to solve the crime until… This mystery is a tribute to *Silver Blaze* and the great racetrack stories of Damon Runyon.

The Box of Cards. A brother and a sister from a strict religious family disappear. The parents are alarmed, but Scotland Yard says they are just off sowing their wild oats. A horrific, gruesome package arrives in the post, and it becomes clear that a terrible crime is in process. Sherlock Holmes is called in to help. A tribute to *The Cardboard Box*.

The Yellow Farce. Sherlock Holmes is sent to Japan. The war between Russia and Japan is raging. Alliances between countries in these years before World War I are fragile, and any misstep could plunge the world into Armageddon. The wife of the British ambassador is suspected of being a Russian agent. Join Holmes and Watson as they travel around the world to Japan. Inspired by *The Yellow Face*.

The Stock Market Murders. A young man's friend has gone missing. Two more bodies of young men turn up. All are tied to The City and to one of the greatest frauds ever visited upon the citizens of England. The story is based on the true story of James Whitaker Wright and is inspired by, *The Stock Broker's Clerk*. Any resemblance of the villain to a certain American political figure is entirely coincidental.

The Glorious Yacht. On the night of April 12, 1912, off the coast of Newfoundland, one of the greatest disasters of all time took place – the Unsinkable Titanic struck an iceberg and sank with a horrendous loss of life. The news of the disaster leads Holmes and Watson to reminisce about one of their earliest adventures. It began as a sailing race and ended as a tale of murder, kidnapping, piracy, and survival through a tempest. A tribute to *The Gloria Scott*.

 ***A Most Grave Ritual.*** In 1649, King Charles I escaped and made a desperate run for Continent. Did he leave behind a vast fortune? The patriarch of an ancient Royalist family dies in the courtyard, and the locals believe that the headless ghost of the king did him in. The police accuse his son of murder. Sherlock Holmes is hired to exonerate the lad. A tribute to *The Musgrave Ritual.*

 ***The Spy Gate Liars.*** Dr. Watson receives an urgent telegram telling him that Sherlock Holmes is in France and near death. He rushes to aid his dear friend, only to find that what began as a doctor's house call has turned into yet another adventure as Sherlock Holmes races to keep an unknown ruthless murderer from dispatching yet another former German army officer. A tribute to *The Reigate Squires.*

 ***The Cuckold Man*** Colonel James Barclay needs the help of Sherlock Holmes. His exceptionally beautiful, but much younger, wife has disappeared, and foul play is suspected. Has she been kidnapped and held for ransom? Or is she in the clutches of a deviant monster? The story is a tribute not only to the original mystery, *The Crooked Man,* but also to the biblical story of King David and Bathsheba.

 ***The Impatient Dissidents.*** In March 1881, the Czar of Russia was assassinated by anarchists. That summer, an attempt was made to murder his daughter, Maria, the wife of England's Prince Alfred. A Russian Count is found dead in a hospital in London. Scotland Yard and the Home Office arrive at 221B and enlist the help of Sherlock Holmes to track down the killers and stop them. This new mystery is a tribute to *The Resident Patient.*

The Grecian, Earned. This story picks up where *The Greek Interpreter* left off. The villains of that story were murdered in Budapest, and so Holmes and Watson set off in search of "the Grecian girl" to solve the mystery. What they discover is a massive plot involving the re-birth of the Olympic games in 1896 and a colorful cast of characters at home and on the Continent.

The Three Rhodes Not Taken. Oxford University is famous for its passionate pursuit of learning. The Rhodes Scholarship has been recently established, and some men are prepared to lie, steal, slander, and, maybe murder, in the pursuit of it. Sherlock Holmes is called upon to track down a thief who has stolen vital documents pertaining to the winner of the scholarship, but what will he do when the prime suspect is found dead? A tribute to *The Three Students.*

The Naval Knaves. On September 15, 1894, an anarchist attempted to bomb the Greenwich Observatory. He failed, but the attempt led Sherlock Holmes into an intricate web of spies, foreign naval officers, and a beautiful princess. Once again, suspicion landed on poor Percy Phelps, now working in a senior position in the Admiralty, and once again Holmes has to use both his powers of deduction and raw courage to not only rescue Percy but to prevent an unspeakable disaster. A tribute to *The Naval Treaty.*

A Scandal in Trumplandia. NOT a new mystery but a political satire. The story is a parody of the much-loved original story, *A Scandal in Bohemia*, with the character of the King of Bohemia replaced by you-know-who. If you enjoy both political satire and Sherlock Holmes, you will get a chuckle out of this new story.

Sherlock and Barack. This is NOT a new Sherlock Holmes Mystery. It is a Sherlockian research monograph. Why did Barack Obama win in November 2012? Why did Mitt Romney lose? Pundits and political scientists have offered countless reasons. This book reveals the truth - The Sherlock Holmes Factor. Had it not been for Sherlock Holmes, Mitt Romney would be president.

From The Beryl Coronet to Vimy Ridge. This is NOT a New Sherlock Holmes Mystery. It is a monograph of Sherlockian research. This new monograph in the Great Game of Sherlockian scholarship argues that there was a Sherlock Holmes factor in the causes of World War I... and that it is secretly revealed in the *roman a clef* story that we know as *The Adventure of the Beryl Coronet.*

The Binomial Asteroid Problem. The deadly final encounter between Professor Moriarty and Sherlock Holmes took place at Reichenbach Falls on 4 May 1891. But when was their first encounter? When did Holmes first come to know that there was an evil genius behind a massive web of crime? This new story answers that question. What began with nothing more than a stolen Gladstone bag on wheels quickly escalates into murder and more. And if Holmes and Watson do not move fast enough, it could become much worse. This new story is a tribute -- a 'prequal' -- to the Canonical story of *The Adventure of the Final Problem.*

Reverend Ezekiel Black—'The Sherlock Holmes of the American West'—Mystery Stories.

A Scarlet Trail of Murder. At ten o'clock on Sunday morning, the twenty-second of October, 1882, in an abandoned house in the West Bottom of Kansas City, a fellow named Jasper Harrison did not wake up. His inability to do was the result of his having had his throat cut. The Reverend Mr. Ezekiel Black, a part-time Methodist minister and an itinerant US Marshall, is called in. This original western mystery was inspired by the great Sherlock Holmes classic, *A Study in Scarlet.*

The Brand of the Flying Four. This case all began one quiet evening in a room in Kansas City. A few weeks later, a gruesome murder, took place in Denver. By the time Rev. Black had solved the mystery, justice, of the frontier variety, not the courtroom, had been meted out. The story is inspired by *The Sign of the Four* by Arthur Conan Doyle, and like that story, it combines murder most foul, and romance most enticing.

Collection Sets for eBooks and paperback are available at *40% off the price of buying them separately.*

Collection One
The Sign of the Third
The Hudson Valley Mystery
A Case of Identity Theft
The Bald-Headed Trust
Studying Scarlet
The Mystery of the Five Oranges

Collection Two
A Sandal from East Anglia
The Man Who Was Twisted
   But Hip
The Blue Belt Buckle
The Spectred Bat

Collection Three
The Engineer's Mom
The Notable Bachelorette
The Beryl Anarchists
The Coiffured Bitches

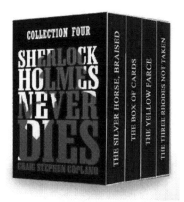

Collection Four

The Silver Horse, Braised
The Box of Cards
The Yellow Farce
The Three Rhodes Not Taken

Collection Five

The Stock Market Murders
The Glorious Yacht
The Most Grave Ritual
The Spy Gate Liars

Collection Six

The Cuckold Man
The Impatient Dissidents
The Grecian, Earned
The Three Rhodes Not
    Taken

The Sign of the Four

The Original Sherlock Holmes Story

Sir Arthur Conan Doyle

1 The Science of Deduction

Sherlock Holmes took his bottle from the corner of the mantel-piece and his hypodermic syringe from its neat morocco case. With his long, white, nervous fingers he adjusted the delicate needle, and rolled back his left shirt-cuff. For some little time his eyes rested thoughtfully upon the sinewy forearm and wrist all dotted and scarred with innumerable puncture-marks. Finally he thrust the sharp point home, pressed down the tiny piston, and sank back into the velvet-lined arm-chair with a long sigh of satisfaction.

Three times a day for many months I had witnessed this performance, but custom had not reconciled my mind to it. On the contrary, from day to day I had become more irritable at the sight, and my conscience swelled nightly within me at the thought that I had lacked the courage to protest. Again and again I had registered a vow that I should deliver my soul upon the subject, but there was that in the cool, nonchalant air of my companion which made him the last man with whom one would care to take anything approaching to a liberty. His great powers, his masterly manner, and the experience which I had had of his many extraordinary qualities, all made me diffident and backward in crossing him.

Yet upon that afternoon, whether it was the Beaune which I had taken with my lunch, or the additional exasperation produced by the extreme deliberation of his manner, I suddenly felt that I could hold out no longer.

"Which is it to-day?" I asked,--"morphine or cocaine?"

He raised his eyes languidly from the old black-letter volume which he had opened. "It is cocaine," he said,--"a seven-per-cent. solution. Would you care to try it?"

"No, indeed," I answered, brusquely. "My constitution has not got over the Afghan campaign yet. I cannot afford to throw any extra strain upon it."

He smiled at my vehemence. "Perhaps you are right, Watson," he said. "I suppose that its influence is physically a bad one. I find it, however, so transcendently stimulating and clarifying to the mind that its secondary action is a matter of small moment."

"But consider!" I said, earnestly. "Count the cost! Your brain may, as you say, be roused and excited, but it is a pathological and morbid process, which involves increased tissue-change and may at last leave a permanent weakness. You know, too, what a black reaction comes upon you. Surely the game is hardly worth the candle. Why should you, for a mere passing pleasure, risk the loss of those great powers with which you have been endowed? Remember that I speak not only as one comrade to another, but as a medical man to one for whose constitution he is to some extent answerable."

He did not seem offended. On the contrary, he put his finger-tips together and leaned his elbows on the arms of his chair, like one who has a relish for conversation.

"My mind," he said, "rebels at stagnation. Give me problems, give me work, give me the most abstruse cryptogram or the most intricate analysis, and I am in my own proper atmosphere. I can dispense then with artificial stimulants. But I abhor the dull routine of existence. I crave for mental exaltation. That is why I have chosen my own particular profession,--or rather created it, for I am the only one in the world."

"The only unofficial detective?" I said, raising my eyebrows.

"The only unofficial consulting detective," he answered. "I am the last and highest court of appeal in detection. When Gregson or Lestrade or Athelney Jones are out of their depths--which, by the way, is their normal state--the matter is laid before me. I examine the data, as an expert, and pronounce a specialist's opinion. I claim no credit in such cases. My name figures in no newspaper. The work itself, the pleasure of finding a field for my peculiar powers, is my highest reward. But you have yourself had some experience of my methods of work in the Jefferson Hope case."

"Yes, indeed," said I, cordially. "I was never so struck by anything in my life. I even embodied it in a small brochure with the somewhat fantastic title of 'A Study in Scarlet.'"

He shook his head sadly. "I glanced over it," said he. "Honestly, I cannot congratulate you upon it. Detection is, or ought to be, an exact science, and should be treated in the same cold and unemotional manner. You have attempted to tinge it with romanticism, which produces much the same effect as if you worked a love-story or an elopement into the fifth proposition of Euclid."

"But the romance was there," I remonstrated. "I could not tamper with the facts."

"Some facts should be suppressed, or at least a just sense of proportion should be observed in treating them. The only point in the case which deserved mention was the curious analytical reasoning from effects to causes by which I succeeded in unraveling it."

I was annoyed at this criticism of a work which had been specially designed to please him. I confess, too, that I was irritated by the egotism which seemed to demand that every line of my pamphlet should be devoted to his own special doings. More than once during the years that I had lived with him in Baker Street I had observed that a small vanity underlay my companion's quiet and didactic manner. I made no remark, however, but sat nursing my wounded leg. I had a Jezail bullet through it some time before, and, though it did not prevent me from walking, it ached wearily at every change of the weather.

"My practice has extended recently to the Continent," said Holmes, after a while, filling up his old brier-root pipe. "I was consulted last week by Francois Le Villard, who, as you probably know, has come rather to the front lately in the French detective service. He has all the Celtic power of quick intuition, but he is deficient in the wide range of exact knowledge which is essential to the higher developments of his art. The case was concerned with a will, and possessed some features of interest. I was able to refer him to two parallel cases, the one at Riga in 1857, and the other at St. Louis in 1871, which have suggested to him the true solution. Here is the letter which I had this morning acknowledging my assistance." He tossed over, as he spoke, a crumpled sheet of foreign notepaper. I glanced my eyes down it, catching a profusion of notes of admiration, with stray "magnifiques," "coup-de-maitres," and "tours-de-force," all testifying to the ardent admiration of the Frenchman.

"He speaks as a pupil to his master," said I.

"Oh, he rates my assistance too highly," said Sherlock Holmes, lightly. "He has considerable gifts himself. He possesses two out of the three qualities necessary for the ideal detective. He has the power of observation and that of deduction. He is only wanting in knowledge; and that may come in time. He is now translating my small works into French."

"Your works?"

"Oh, didn't you know?" he cried, laughing. "Yes, I have been guilty of several monographs. They are all upon technical subjects. Here, for example, is one 'Upon the Distinction between the Ashes of the Various Tobaccoes.' In it I enumerate a hundred and forty forms of cigar-, cigarette-, and pipe-tobacco, with colored plates illustrating the difference in the ash. It is a point which is continually turning up in criminal trials, and which is sometimes of supreme importance as a clue. If you can say definitely, for example, that some murder has been done by a man who was smoking an Indian lunkah, it obviously narrows your field of search. To the trained eye there is as much difference between the black ash of a Trichinopoly and the white fluff of bird's-eye as there is between a cabbage and a potato."

"You have an extraordinary genius for minutiae," I remarked.

"I appreciate their importance. Here is my monograph upon the tracing of footsteps, with some remarks upon the uses of plaster of Paris as a preserver of impresses. Here, too, is a curious little work upon the influence of a trade upon the form of the hand, with lithotypes of the hands of slaters, sailors, corkcutters, compositors, weavers, and diamond-polishers. That is a matter of great practical interest to the scientific detective,--especially in cases of unclaimed bodies, or in discovering the antecedents of criminals. But I weary you with my hobby."

"Not at all," I answered, earnestly. "It is of the greatest interest to me, especially since I have had the opportunity of observing your practical application of it. But you spoke just now of observation and deduction. Surely the one to some extent implies the other."

"Why, hardly," he answered, leaning back luxuriously in his arm-chair, and sending up thick blue wreaths from his pipe. "For example, observation shows me that you have been to the Wigmore Street Post-Office this morning, but deduction lets me know that when there you dispatched a telegram."

"Right!" said I. "Right on both points! But I confess that I don't see how you arrived at it. It was a sudden impulse upon my part, and I have mentioned it to no one."

"It is simplicity itself," he remarked, chuckling at my surprise,--"so absurdly simple that an explanation is superfluous; and yet it may serve to define the limits of observation and of deduction. Observation tells me that you have a little reddish mould adhering to your instep. Just opposite the Seymour Street Office they have taken up the pavement and thrown up some earth which lies in such a way that it is difficult to avoid treading in it in entering. The earth is of this peculiar reddish tint which is found, as far as I know, nowhere else in the neighborhood. So much is observation. The rest is deduction."

"How, then, did you deduce the telegram?"

"Why, of course I knew that you had not written a letter, since I sat opposite to you all morning. I see also in your open desk there that you have a sheet of stamps and a thick bundle of post-cards. What could you go into the post-office for, then, but to send a wire? Eliminate all other factors, and the one which remains must be the truth."

"In this case it certainly is so," I replied, after a little thought. "The thing, however, is, as you say, of the simplest.

Would you think me impertinent if I were to put your theories to a more severe test?"

"On the contrary," he answered, "it would prevent me from taking a second dose of cocaine. I should be delighted to look into any problem which you might submit to me."

"I have heard you say that it is difficult for a man to have any object in daily use without leaving the impress of his individuality upon it in such a way that a trained observer might read it. Now, I have here a watch which has recently come into my possession. Would you have the kindness to let me have an opinion upon the character or habits of the late owner?"

I handed him over the watch with some slight feeling of amusement in my heart, for the test was, as I thought, an impossible one, and I intended it as a lesson against the somewhat dogmatic tone which he occasionally assumed. He balanced the watch in his hand, gazed hard at the dial, opened the back, and examined the works, first with his naked eyes and then with a powerful convex lens. I could hardly keep from smiling at his crestfallen face when he finally snapped the case to and handed it back.

"There are hardly any data," he remarked. "The watch has been recently cleaned, which robs me of my most suggestive facts."

"You are right," I answered. "It was cleaned before being sent to me." In my heart I accused my companion of putting forward a most lame and impotent excuse to cover his failure. What data could he expect from an uncleaned watch?

"Though unsatisfactory, my research has not been entirely barren," he observed, staring up at the ceiling with dreamy, lack-lustre eyes. "Subject to your correction, I should judge that the watch belonged to your elder brother, who inherited it from your father."

"That you gather, no doubt, from the H. W. upon the back?"

"Quite so. The W. suggests your own name. The date of the watch is nearly fifty years back, and the initials are as old as the watch: so it was made for the last generation. Jewelry usually descends to the eldest son, and he is most likely to have the same name as the father. Your father has, if I remember right, been dead many years. It has, therefore, been in the hands of your eldest brother."

"Right, so far," said I. "Anything else?"

"He was a man of untidy habits,--very untidy and careless. He was left with good prospects, but he threw away his chances, lived for some time in poverty with occasional short intervals of prosperity, and finally, taking to drink, he died. That is all I can gather."

I sprang from my chair and limped impatiently about the room with considerable bitterness in my heart.

"This is unworthy of you, Holmes," I said. "I could not have believed that you would have descended to this. You have made inquires into the history of my unhappy brother, and you now pretend to deduce this knowledge in some fanciful way. You cannot expect me to believe that you have read all this from his old watch! It is unkind, and, to speak plainly, has a touch of charlatanism in it."

"My dear doctor," said he, kindly, "pray accept my apologies. Viewing the matter as an abstract problem, I had forgotten how personal and painful a thing it might be to you. I assure you, however, that I never even knew that you had a brother until you handed me the watch."

"Then how in the name of all that is wonderful did you get these facts? They are absolutely correct in every particular."

"Ah, that is good luck. I could only say what was the balance of probability. I did not at all expect to be so accurate."

"But it was not mere guess-work?"

"No, no: I never guess. It is a shocking habit,-- destructive to the logical faculty. What seems strange to you is only so because you do not follow my train of thought or observe the small facts upon which large inferences may depend. For example, I began by stating that your brother was careless. When you observe the lower part of that watch-case you notice that it is not only dinted in two places, but it is cut and marked all over from the habit of keeping other hard objects, such as coins or keys, in the same pocket. Surely it is no great feat to assume that a man who treats a fifty-guinea watch so cavalierly must be a careless man. Neither is it a very far-fetched inference that a man who inherits one article of such value is pretty well provided for in other respects."

I nodded, to show that I followed his reasoning.

"It is very customary for pawnbrokers in England, when they take a watch, to scratch the number of the ticket with a pin-point upon the inside of the case. It is more handy than a label, as there is no risk of the number being lost or transposed. There are no less than four such numbers visible to my lens on the inside of this case. Inference,--that your brother was often at low water. Secondary inference,--that he had occasional bursts of prosperity, or he could not have redeemed the pledge. Finally, I ask you to look at the inner plate, which contains the key-hole. Look at the thousands of scratches all round the hole,--marks where the key has slipped. What sober man's key could have scored those grooves? But you will never see a drunkard's watch without them. He winds it at night, and he leaves these traces of his unsteady hand. Where is the mystery in all this?"

"It is as clear as daylight," I answered. "I regret the injustice which I did you. I should have had more faith in your marvellous faculty. May I ask whether you have any professional inquiry on foot at present?"

"None. Hence the cocaine. I cannot live without brain-work. What else is there to live for? Stand at the window here. Was ever such a dreary, dismal, unprofitable world? See how the yellow fog swirls down the street and drifts across the dun-colored houses. What could be more hopelessly prosaic and material? What is the use of having powers, doctor, when one has no field upon which to exert them? Crime is commonplace, existence is commonplace, and no qualities save those which are commonplace have any function upon earth."

I had opened my mouth to reply to this tirade, when with a crisp knock our landlady entered, bearing a card upon the brass salver.

"A young lady for you, sir," she said, addressing my companion.

"Miss Mary Morstan," he read. "Hum! I have no recollection of the name. Ask the young lady to step up, Mrs. Hudson. Don't go, doctor. I should prefer that you remain."

2 The Statement of the Case

Miss Morstan entered the room with a firm step and an outward composure of manner. She was a blonde young lady, small, dainty, well gloved, and dressed in the most perfect taste. There was, however, a plainness and simplicity about her costume which bore with it a suggestion of limited means. The dress was a somber grayish beige, untrimmed and unbraided, and she wore a small turban of the same dull hue, relieved only by a suspicion of white feather in the side. Her face had neither regularity of feature nor beauty of complexion, but her expression was sweet and amiable, and her large blue eyes were singularly spiritual and sympathetic. In an experience of women which extends over many nations and three separate continents, I have never looked upon a face which gave a clearer promise of a refined and sensitive nature. I could not but observe that as she took the seat which Sherlock Holmes placed for her, her lip trembled, her hand quivered, and she showed every sign of intense inward agitation.

"I have come to you, Mr. Holmes," she said, "because you once enabled my employer, Mrs. Cecil Forrester, to unravel a little domestic complication. She was much impressed by your kindness and skill."

"Mrs. Cecil Forrester," he repeated thoughtfully. "I believe that I was of some slight service to her. The case, however, as I remember it, was a very simple one."

"She did not think so. But at least you cannot say the same of mine. I can hardly imagine anything more strange, more utterly inexplicable, than the situation in which I find myself."

Holmes rubbed his hands, and his eyes glistened. He leaned forward in his chair with an expression of extraordinary concentration upon his clear-cut, hawk like features. "State your case," said he, in brisk, business tones.

I felt that my position was an embarrassing one. "You will, I am sure, excuse me," I said, rising from my chair.

To my surprise, the young lady held up her gloved hand to detain me. "If your friend," she said, "would be good enough to stop, he might be of inestimable service to me."

I relapsed into my chair.

"Briefly," she continued, "the facts are these. My father was an officer in an Indian regiment who sent me home when I was quite a child. My mother was dead, and I had no relative in England. I was placed, however, in a comfortable boarding establishment at Edinburgh, and there I remained until I was seventeen years of age. In the year 1878 my father, who was senior captain of his regiment, obtained twelve months' leave and came home. He telegraphed to me from London that he had arrived all safe, and directed me to come down at once, giving the Langham Hotel as his address. His message, as I remember, was full of kindness and love. On reaching London I drove to the Langham, and was informed that Captain Morstan was staying there, but that he had gone out the night before and had not yet returned. I waited all day without news of him. That night, on the advice of the manager of the hotel, I communicated with the police, and next morning we advertised in all the papers. Our inquiries led to no result; and from that day to this no word has ever been heard of my unfortunate father. He came home with his heart full of hope, to find some peace, some comfort, and instead--" She put her hand to her throat, and a choking sob cut short the sentence.

"The date?" asked Holmes, opening his note-book.

"He disappeared upon the 3rd of December, 1878,--nearly ten years ago."

"His luggage?"

"Remained at the hotel. There was nothing in it to suggest a clue,--some clothes, some books, and a considerable number of curiosities from the Andaman Islands. He had been one of the officers in charge of the convict-guard there."

"Had he any friends in town?"

"Only one that we know of,--Major Sholto, of his own regiment, the 34th Bombay Infantry. The major had retired some little time before, and lived at Upper Norwood. We communicated with him, of course, but he did not even know that his brother officer was in England."

"A singular case," remarked Holmes.

"I have not yet described to you the most singular part. About six years ago--to be exact, upon the 4th of May, 1882--an advertisement appeared in the Times asking for the address of Miss Mary Morstan and stating that it would be to her advantage to come forward. There was no name or address appended. I had at that time just entered the family of Mrs. Cecil Forrester in the capacity of governess. By her advice I published my address in the advertisement column. The same day there arrived through the post a small card-board box addressed to me, which I found to contain a very large and lustrous pearl. No word of writing was enclosed. Since then every year upon the same date there has always appeared a similar box, containing a similar pearl, without any clue as to the sender. They have been pronounced by an expert to be of a rare variety and of considerable value. You can see for yourselves that they are very handsome." She opened a flat box as she spoke, and showed me six of the finest pearls that I had ever seen.

"Your statement is most interesting," said Sherlock Holmes. "Has anything else occurred to you?"

"Yes, and no later than to-day. That is why I have come to you. This morning I received this letter, which you will perhaps read for yourself."

"Thank you," said Holmes. "The envelope too, please. Postmark, London, S.W. Date, July 7. Hum! Man's thumb-mark on corner,--probably postman. Best quality paper. Envelopes at sixpence a packet. Particular man in his stationery. No address. 'Be at the third pillar from the left outside the Lyceum Theatre to-night at seven o'clock. If you are distrustful, bring two friends. You are a wronged woman, and shall have justice. Do not bring police. If you do, all will be in vain. Your unknown friend.' Well, really, this is a very pretty little mystery. What do you intend to do, Miss Morstan?"

"That is exactly what I want to ask you."

"Then we shall most certainly go. You and I and--yes, why, Dr. Watson is the very man. Your correspondent says two friends. He and I have worked together before."

"But would he come?" she asked, with something appealing in her voice and expression.

"I should be proud and happy," said I, fervently, "if I can be of any service."

"You are both very kind," she answered. "I have led a

retired life, and have no friends whom I could appeal to. If I am here at six it will do, I suppose?"

"You must not be later," said Holmes. "There is one other point, however. Is this handwriting the same as that upon the pearl-box addresses?"

"I have them here," she answered, producing half a dozen pieces of paper.

"You are certainly a model client. You have the correct intuition. Let us see, now." He spread out the papers upon the table, and gave little darting glances from one to the other. "They are disguised hands, except the letter," he said, presently, "but there can be no question as to the authorship. See how the irrepressible Greek e will break out, and see the twirl of the final s. They are undoubtedly by the same person. I should not like to suggest false hopes, Miss Morstan, but is there any resemblance between this hand and that of your father?"

"Nothing could be more unlike."

"I expected to hear you say so. We shall look out for you, then, at six. Pray allow me to keep the papers. I may look into the matter before then. It is only half-past three. Au revoir, then."

"Au revoir," said our visitor, and, with a bright, kindly glance from one to the other of us, she replaced her pearl-box in her bosom and hurried away. Standing at the window, I watched her walking briskly down the street, until the gray turban and white feather were but a speck in the somber crowd.

"What a very attractive woman!" I exclaimed, turning to my companion.

He had lit his pipe again, and was leaning back with drooping eyelids. "Is she?" he said, languidly. "I did not observe."

"You really are an automaton,--a calculating-machine!" I cried. "There is something positively inhuman in you at times."

He smiled gently. "It is of the first importance," he said, "not to allow your judgment to be biased by personal qualities. A client is to me a mere unit,--a factor in a problem. The emotional qualities are antagonistic to clear reasoning. I assure you that the most winning woman I ever knew was hanged for poisoning three little children for their insurance-money, and the most repellant man of my acquaintance is a philanthropist who has spent nearly a quarter of a million upon the London poor."

"In this case, however--"

"I never make exceptions. An exception disproves the rule. Have you ever had occasion to study character in handwriting? What do you make of this fellow's scribble?"

"It is legible and regular," I answered. "A man of business habits and some force of character."

Holmes shook his head. "Look at his long letters," he said. "They hardly rise above the common herd. That d might be an a, and that l an e. Men of character always differentiate their long letters, however illegibly they may write. There is vacillation in his k's and self-esteem in his capitals. I am going out now. I have some few references to make. Let me recommend this book,--one of the most remarkable ever penned. It is Winwood Reade's 'Martyrdom of Man.' I shall be back in an hour."

I sat in the window with the volume in my hand, but my

thoughts were far from the daring speculations of the writer. My mind ran upon our late visitor,--her smiles, the deep rich tones of her voice, the strange mystery which overhung her life. If she were seventeen at the time of her father's disappearance she must be seven-and-twenty now,--a sweet age, when youth has lost its self-consciousness and become a little sobered by experience. So I sat and mused, until such dangerous thoughts came into my head that I hurried away to my desk and plunged furiously into the latest treatise upon pathology. What was I, an army surgeon with a weak leg and a weaker banking-account, that I should dare to think of such things? She was a unit, a factor,--nothing more.

If my future were black, it was better surely to face it like a man than to attempt to brighten it by mere will-o'-the-wisps of the imagination

3 In Quest of a Solution

It was half-past five before Holmes returned. He was bright, eager, and in excellent spirits,--a mood which in his case alternated with fits of the blackest depression.

"There is no great mystery in this matter," he said, taking the cup of tea which I had poured out for him. "The facts appear to admit of only one explanation."

"What! you have solved it already?"

"Well, that would be too much to say. I have discovered a suggestive fact, that is all. It is, however, VERY suggestive. The details are still to be added. I have just found, on consulting the back files of the Times, that Major Sholto, of Upper Norword, late of the 34th Bombay Infantry, died upon the 28th of April, 1882."

"I may be very obtuse, Holmes, but I fail to see what this suggests."

"No? You surprise me. Look at it in this way, then. Captain Morstan disappears. The only person in London whom he could have visited is Major Sholto. Major Sholto denies having heard that he was in London. Four years later Sholto dies. WITHIN A WEEK OF HIS DEATH Captain Morstan's daughter receives a valuable present, which is repeated from year to year, and now culminates in a letter which describes her as a wronged woman. What wrong can it refer to except this deprivation of her father? And why should the presents begin immediately after Sholto's death, unless it is that Sholto's heir knows something of the mystery and desires to make compensation? Have you any alternative theory which will meet the facts?"

"But what a strange compensation! And how strangely made! Why, too, should he write a letter now, rather than six years ago? Again, the letter speaks of giving her justice. What justice can she have? It is too much to suppose that her father is still alive. There is no other injustice in her case that you know of."

"There are difficulties; there are certainly difficulties," said Sherlock Holmes, pensively. "But our expedition of to-night will solve them all. Ah, here is a four-wheeler, and Miss Morstan is inside. Are you all ready? Then we had better go down, for it is a little past the hour."

I picked up my hat and my heaviest stick, but I observed that Holmes took his revolver from his drawer and slipped it into his pocket. It was clear that he thought that our night's work might be a serious one.

Miss Morstan was muffled in a dark cloak, and her sensitive face was composed, but pale. She must have been more than woman if she did not feel some uneasiness at the strange enterprise upon which we were embarking, yet her self-control was perfect, and she readily answered the few additional questions which Sherlock Holmes put to her.

"Major Sholto was a very particular friend of papa's," she said. "His letters were full of allusions to the major. He and papa were in command of the troops at the Andaman Islands, so they were thrown a great deal together. By the way, a curious paper was found in papa's desk which no one could understand. I don't suppose that it is of the slightest importance, but I thought you might care to see it, so I brought it with me. It is here."

Holmes unfolded the paper carefully and smoothed it out upon his knee. He then very methodically examined it all over with his double lens.

"It is paper of native Indian manufacture," he remarked. "It has at some time been pinned to a board. The diagram upon it appears to be a plan of part of a large building with numerous halls, corridors, and passages. At one point is a small cross done in red ink, and above it is '3.37 from left,' in faded pencil-writing. In the left-hand corner is a curious hieroglyphic like four crosses in a line with their arms touching. Beside it is written, in very rough and coarse characters, 'The sign of the four,--Jonathan Small, Mahomet Singh, Abdullah Khan, Dost Akbar.' No, I confess that I do not see how this bears upon the matter. Yet it is evidently a document of importance. It has been kept carefully in a pocket-book; for the one side is as clean as the other."

"It was in his pocket-book that we found it."

"Preserve it carefully, then, Miss Morstan, for it may prove to be of use to us. I begin to suspect that this matter may turn out to be much deeper and more subtle than I at first supposed. I must reconsider my ideas." He leaned back in the cab, and I could see by his drawn brow and his vacant eye that he was thinking intently. Miss Morstan and I chatted in an undertone about our present expedition and its possible outcome, but our companion maintained his impenetrable reserve until the end of our journey.

It was a September evening, and not yet seven o'clock, but the day had been a dreary one, and a dense drizzly fog lay low upon the great city. Mud-colored clouds drooped sadly over the muddy streets. Down the Strand the lamps were but misty splotches of diffused light which threw a feeble circular glimmer upon the slimy pavement. The yellow glare from the shop-windows streamed out into the steamy, vaporous air, and threw a murky, shifting radiance across the crowded thoroughfare. There was, to my mind, something eerie and ghost-like in the endless procession of faces which flitted across these narrow bars of light,--sad faces and glad, haggard and merry. Like all human kind, they flitted from the gloom into the light, and so back into the gloom once more. I am not subject to impressions, but the dull, heavy evening, with the strange business upon which we were engaged, combined to make me nervous and depressed. I could see from Miss Morstan's manner that she was suffering from the same feeling. Holmes alone could rise superior to petty influences. He held his open note-book upon his knee, and from time to time he jotted down figures and memoranda in the light of his pocket-lantern.

At the Lyceum Theatre the crowds were already thick at the side-entrances. In front a continuous stream of hansoms and four-wheelers were rattling up, discharging their cargoes of shirt-fronted men and beshawled, bediamonded women. We had hardly reached the third pillar, which was our rendezvous, before a small, dark, brisk man in the dress of a coachman accosted us.

"Are you the parties who come with Miss Morstan?" he asked.

"I am Miss Morstan, and these two gentlemen are my friends," said she.

He bent a pair of wonderfully penetrating and questioning eyes upon us. "You will excuse me, miss," he said with a certain dogged manner, "but I was to ask you to give me your word that neither of your companions is a police-officer."

"I give you my word on that," she answered.

He gave a shrill whistle, on which a street Arab led across a four-wheeler and opened the door. The man who had addressed us mounted to the box, while we took our places inside. We had hardly done so before the driver whipped up his horse, and we plunged away at a furious pace through the foggy streets.

The situation was a curious one. We were driving to an unknown place, on an unknown errand. Yet our invitation was either a complete hoax,--which was an inconceivable hypothesis,--or else we had good reason to think that important issues might hang upon our journey. Miss Morstan's demeanor was as resolute and collected as ever. I endeavored to cheer and amuse her by reminiscences of my adventures in Afghanistan; but, to tell the truth, I was myself so excited at our situation and so curious as to our destination that my stories were slightly involved. To this day she declares that I told her one moving anecdote as to how a musket looked into my tent at the dead of night, and how I fired a double-barreled tiger cub at it. At first I had some idea as to the direction in which we were driving; but soon, what with our pace, the fog, and my own limited knowledge of London, I lost my bearings, and knew nothing, save that we seemed to be going a very long way. Sherlock Holmes was never at fault, however, and he muttered the names as the cab rattled through squares and in and out by tortuous by-streets.

"Rochester Row," said he. "Now Vincent Square. Now we come out on the Vauxhall Bridge Road. We are making for the Surrey side, apparently. Yes, I thought so. Now we are on the bridge. You can catch glimpses of the river."

We did indeed get a fleeting view of a stretch of the Thames with the lamps shining upon the broad, silent

128

water; but our cab dashed on, and was soon involved in a labyrinth of streets upon the other side.

"Wordsworth Road," said my companion. "Priory Road. Lark Hall Lane. Stockwell Place. Robert Street. Cold Harbor Lane. Our quest does not appear to take us to very fashionable regions."

We had, indeed, reached a questionable and forbidding neighborhood. Long lines of dull brick houses were only relieved by the coarse glare and tawdry brilliancy of public houses at the corner. Then came rows of two-storied villas each with a fronting of miniature garden, and then again interminable lines of new staring brick buildings,--the monster tentacles which the giant city was throwing out into the country. At last the cab drew up at the third house in a new terrace. None of the other houses were inhabited, and that at which we stopped was as dark as its neighbors, save for a single glimmer in the kitchen window. On our knocking, however, the door was instantly thrown open by a Hindu servant clad in a yellow turban, white loose-fitting clothes, and a yellow sash. There was something strangely incongruous in this Oriental figure framed in the commonplace door-way of a third-rate suburban dwelling-house.

"The Sahib awaits you," said he, and even as he spoke there came a high piping voice from some inner room. "Show them in to me, khitmutgar," it cried. "Show them straight in to me."

4 The Story of the Bald-Headed Man

We followed the Indian down a sordid and common passage, ill lit and worse furnished, until he came to a door upon the right, which he threw open. A blaze of yellow light streamed out upon us, and in the center of the glare there stood a small man with a very high head, a bristle of red hair all round the fringe of it, and a bald, shining scalp which shot out from among it like a mountain-peak from fir-trees. He writhed his hands together as he stood, and his features were in a perpetual jerk, now smiling, now scowling, but never for an instant in repose. Nature had given him a pendulous lip, and a too visible line of yellow and irregular teeth, which he strove feebly to conceal by constantly passing his hand over the lower part of his face. In spite of his obtrusive baldness, he gave the impression of youth. In point of fact he had just turned his thirtieth year.

"Your servant, Miss Morstan," he kept repeating, in a thin, high voice. "Your servant, gentlemen. Pray step into my little sanctum. A small place, miss, but furnished to my own liking. An oasis of art in the howling desert of South London."

We were all astonished by the appearance of the apartment into which he invited us. In that sorry house it looked as out of place as a diamond of the first water in a setting of brass. The richest and glossiest of curtains and tapestries draped the walls, looped back here and there to expose some richly-mounted painting or Oriental vase. The carpet was of amber-and-black, so soft and so thick that the foot sank pleasantly into it, as into a bed of moss. Two great tiger-skins thrown athwart it increased the suggestion of

Eastern luxury, as did a huge hookah which stood upon a mat in the corner. A lamp in the fashion of a silver dove was hung from an almost invisible golden wire in the center of the room. As it burned it filled the air with a subtle and aromatic odor.

"Mr. Thaddeus Sholto," said the little man, still jerking and smiling. "That is my name. You are Miss Morstan, of course. And these gentlemen--"

"This is Mr. Sherlock Holmes, and this is Dr. Watson."

"A doctor, eh?" cried he, much excited. "Have you your stethoscope? Might I ask you--would you have the kindness? I have grave doubts as to my mitral valve, if you would be so very good. The aortic I may rely upon, but I should value your opinion upon the mitral."

I listened to his heart, as requested, but was unable to find anything amiss, save indeed that he was in an ecstasy of fear, for he shivered from head to foot. "It appears to be normal," I said. "You have no cause for uneasiness."

"You will excuse my anxiety, Miss Morstan," he remarked, airily. "I am a great sufferer, and I have long had suspicions as to that valve. I am delighted to hear that they are unwarranted. Had your father, Miss Morstan, refrained from throwing a strain upon his heart, he might have been alive now."

I could have struck the man across the face, so hot was I at this callous and off-hand reference to so delicate a matter. Miss Morstan sat down, and her face grew white to the lips. "I knew in my heart that he was dead," said she.

"I can give you every information," said he, "and, what is more, I can do you justice; and I will, too, whatever Brother Bartholomew may say. I am so glad to have your friends

131

here, not only as an escort to you, but also as witnesses to what I am about to do and say. The three of us can show a bold front to Brother Bartholomew. But let us have no outsiders,--no police or officials. We can settle everything satisfactorily among ourselves, without any interference. Nothing would annoy Brother Bartholomew more than any publicity." He sat down upon a low settee and blinked at us inquiringly with his weak, watery blue eyes.

"For my part," said Holmes, "whatever you may choose to say will go no further."

I nodded to show my agreement.

"That is well! That is well!" said he. "May I offer you a glass of Chianti, Miss Morstan? Or of Tokay? I keep no other wines. Shall I open a flask? No? Well, then, I trust that you have no objection to tobacco-smoke, to the mild balsamic odor of the Eastern tobacco. I am a little nervous, and I find my hookah an invaluable sedative." He applied a taper to the great bowl, and the smoke bubbled merrily through the rose-water. We sat all three in a semicircle, with our heads advanced, and our chins upon our hands, while the strange, jerky little fellow, with his high, shining head, puffed uneasily in the center.

"When I first determined to make this communication to you," said he, "I might have given you my address, but I feared that you might disregard my request and bring unpleasant people with you. I took the liberty, therefore, of making an appointment in such a way that my man Williams might be able to see you first. I have complete confidence in his discretion, and he had orders, if he were dissatisfied, to proceed no further in the matter. You will excuse these precautions, but I am a man of somewhat retiring, and I might even say refined, tastes, and there is nothing more unaesthetic than a policeman. I have a natural shrinking from all forms of rough materialism. I seldom come in contact with the rough crowd. I live, as you see, with some little atmosphere of elegance around me. I may call myself a patron of the arts. It is my weakness. The landscape is a genuine Corot, and, though a connoisseur might perhaps throw a doubt upon that Salvator Rosa, there cannot be the least question about the Bouguereau. I am partial to the modern French school."

"You will excuse me, Mr. Sholto," said Miss Morstan, "but I am here at your request to learn something which you desire to tell me. It is very late, and I should desire the interview to be as short as possible."

"At the best it must take some time," he answered; "for we shall certainly have to go to Norwood and see Brother Bartholomew. We shall all go and try if we can get the better of Brother Bartholomew. He is very angry with me for taking the course which has seemed right to me. I had quite high words with him last night. You cannot imagine what a terrible fellow he is when he is angry."

"If we are to go to Norwood it would perhaps be as well to start at once," I ventured to remark.

He laughed until his ears were quite red. "That would hardly do," he cried. "I don't know what he would say if I brought you in that sudden way. No, I must prepare you by showing you how we all stand to each other. In the first place, I must tell you that there are several points in the story of which I am myself ignorant. I can only lay the facts before you as far as I know them myself.

"My father was, as you may have guessed, Major John Sholto, once of the Indian army. He retired some eleven years ago, and came to live at Pondicherry Lodge in Upper

Norwood. He had prospered in India, and brought back with him a considerable sum of money, a large collection of valuable curiosities, and a staff of native servants. With these advantages he bought himself a house, and lived in great luxury. My twin-brother Bartholomew and I were the only children.

"I very well remember the sensation which was caused by the disappearance of Captain Morstan. We read the details in the papers, and, knowing that he had been a friend of our father's, we discussed the case freely in his presence. He used to join in our speculations as to what could have happened. Never for an instant did we suspect that he had the whole secret hidden in his own breast,--that of all men he alone knew the fate of Arthur Morstan.

"We did know, however, that some mystery--some positive danger--overhung our father. He was very fearful of going out alone, and he always employed two prize-fighters to act as porters at Pondicherry Lodge. Williams, who drove you to-night, was one of them. He was once light-weight champion of England. Our father would never tell us what it was he feared, but he had a most marked aversion to men with wooden legs. On one occasion he actually fired his revolver at a wooden-legged man, who proved to be a harmless tradesman canvassing for orders. We had to pay a large sum to hush the matter up. My brother and I used to think this a mere whim of my father's, but events have since led us to change our opinion.

"Early in 1882 my father received a letter from India which was a great shock to him. He nearly fainted at the breakfast-table when he opened it, and from that day he sickened to his death. What was in the letter we could never discover, but I could see as he held it that it was short and written in a scrawling hand. He had suffered for years from an enlarged spleen, but he now became rapidly worse, and towards the end of April we were informed that he was beyond all hope, and that he wished to make a last communication to us.

"When we entered his room he was propped up with pillows and breathing heavily. He besought us to lock the door and to come upon either side of the bed. Then, grasping our hands, he made a remarkable statement to us, in a voice which was broken as much by emotion as by pain. I shall try and give it to you in his own very words.

"'I have only one thing,' he said, 'which weighs upon my mind at this supreme moment. It is my treatment of poor Morstan's orphan. The cursed greed which has been my besetting sin through life has withheld from her the treasure, half at least of which should have been hers. And yet I have made no use of it myself,--so blind and foolish a thing is avarice. The mere feeling of possession has been so dear to me that I could not bear to share it with another. See that chaplet dipped with pearls beside the quinine-bottle. Even that I could not bear to part with, although I had got it out with the design of sending it to her. You, my sons, will give her a fair share of the Agra treasure. But send her nothing-- not even the chaplet--until I am gone. After all, men have been as bad as this and have recovered.

"'I will tell you how Morstan died,' he continued. 'He had suffered for years from a weak heart, but he concealed it from every one. I alone knew it. When in India, he and I, through a remarkable chain of circumstances, came into possession of a considerable treasure. I brought it over to England, and on the night of Morstan's arrival he came straight over here to claim his share. He walked over from the station, and was admitted by my faithful Lal Chowdar, who is now dead. Morstan and I had a difference of opinion as to the division of the treasure, and we came to heated words. Morstan had sprung out of his chair in a paroxysm of anger, when he suddenly pressed his hand to his side, his face turned a dusky hue, and he fell backwards, cutting his head against the corner of the treasure-chest. When I stooped over him I found, to my horror, that he was dead.

"'For a long time I sat half distracted, wondering what I should do. My first impulse was, of course, to call for assistance; but I could not but recognize that there was every chance that I would be accused of his murder. His death at the moment of a quarrel, and the gash in his head, would be black against me. Again, an official inquiry could not be made without bringing out some facts about the treasure, which I was particularly anxious to keep secret. He had told me that no soul upon earth knew where he had gone. There seemed to be no necessity why any soul ever should know.

"'I was still pondering over the matter, when, looking up, I saw my servant, Lal Chowdar, in the doorway. He stole in and bolted the door behind him. "Do not fear, Sahib," he said. "No one need know that you have killed him. Let us hide him away, and who is the wiser?" "I did not kill him," said I. Lal Chowdar shook his head and smiled. "I heard it all, Sahib," said he. "I heard you quarrel, and I heard the blow. But my lips are sealed. All are asleep in the house. Let us put him away together." That was enough to decide me. If my own servant could not believe my innocence, how could I hope to make it good before twelve foolish tradesmen in a jury-box? Lal Chowdar and I disposed of the body that night, and within a few days the London papers were full of the mysterious disappearance of Captain Morstan. You will see from what I say that I can hardly be blamed in the matter. My fault lies in the fact that we concealed not only the body, but also the treasure, and that I have clung to Morstan's share as well as to my own. I wish you, therefore, to make restitution. Put your ears down to my mouth. The treasure is hidden in--' At this instant a horrible change came over his expression; his eyes stared wildly, his jaw dropped, and he yelled, in a voice which I can never forget, 'Keep him out! For Christ's sake keep him out!' We both stared round at the window behind us upon which his gaze was fixed. A face was looking in at us out of the darkness. We could see the whitening of the nose where it was pressed against the glass. It was a bearded, hairy face, with wild cruel eyes and an expression of concentrated malevolence. My brother and I rushed towards the window, but the man was gone. When we returned to my father his head had dropped and his pulse had ceased to beat.

"We searched the garden that night, but found no sign of the intruder, save that just under the window a single footmark was visible in the flower-bed. But for that one trace, we might have thought that our imaginations had conjured up that wild, fierce face. We soon, however, had another and a more striking proof that there were secret agencies at work all round us. The window of my father's room was found open in the morning, his cupboards and boxes had been rifled, and upon his chest was fixed a torn piece of paper, with the words 'The sign of the four' scrawled across it. What the phrase meant, or who our secret visitor may have been, we never knew. As far as we can judge, none of my father's property had been actually stolen, though everything had been turned out. My brother and I naturally associated this peculiar incident with the fear which haunted my father during his life;   but it is still a complete mystery to us."

The little man stopped to relight his hookah and puffed thoughtfully for a few moments. We had all sat absorbed, listening to his extraordinary narrative. At the short account of her father's death Miss Morstan had turned deadly white, and for a moment I feared that she was about to faint. She rallied however, on drinking a glass of water which I quietly poured out for her from a Venetian carafe upon the side-table. Sherlock Holmes leaned back in his chair with an abstracted expression and the lids drawn low over his glittering eyes. As I glanced at him I could not but think how on that very day he had   complained bitterly of the commonplaceness of life. Here at least was a problem which would tax his sagacity to the utmost. Mr. Thaddeus Sholto looked from one to the other of us with an obvious pride at the effect which his story had produced, and then continued between the puffs of his overgrown pipe.

"My brother and I," said he, "were, as you may imagine, much excited as to the treasure which my father had spoken of. For weeks and for months we dug and delved in every part of the garden, without discovering its whereabouts. It was maddening to think that the hiding-place was on his very lips at the moment that he died. We could judge the splendor of the missing riches by the chaplet which he had taken out. Over this chaplet my brother Bartholomew and I had some little discussion. The pearls were evidently of great value, and he was averse to part with them, for, between friends, my brother was himself a little inclined to my father's fault. He thought, too, that if we parted with the chaplet it might give rise to gossip and finally bring us into trouble. It was all that I could do to persuade him to   let me find out Miss Morstan's address and send her a detached pearl at   fixed intervals, so that at least she might never feel destitute."

"It was a kindly thought," said our companion, earnestly. "It was extremely good of you."

The little man waved his hand deprecatingly. "We were your trustees," he said. "That was the view which I took of it, though Brother Bartholomew could not altogether see it in that light. We had plenty of money ourselves. I desired no more. Besides, it would have been such bad taste to have treated a young lady in so scurvy a fashion. 'Le mauvais gout mene au crime.' The French have a very neat way of putting these things. Our difference of opinion on this subject went so far that I thought it best to set up rooms for myself: so I left Pondicherry Lodge, taking the old khitmutgar and Williams with me. Yesterday, however, I learn that an event of extreme importance has occurred. The treasure has been discovered. I instantly communicated with Miss Morstan, and it only remains for us to drive out to Norwood and demand our share. I explained my views last night to Brother Bartholomew: so we shall be expected, if not welcome, visitors."

Mr. Thaddeus Sholto ceased, and sat twitching on his luxurious settee. We all remained silent, with our thoughts upon the new development which the mysterious business had taken. Holmes was the first to spring to his feet.

"You have done well, sir, from first to last," said he. "It is possible that we may be able to make you some small return by throwing some light upon that which is still dark to you. But, as Miss Morstan remarked just now, it is late, and we had best put the matter through without delay."

Our new acquaintance very deliberately coiled up the tube of his hookah, and produced from behind a curtain a very long befrogged topcoat with Astrakhan collar and cuffs. This he buttoned tightly up, in spite of the extreme closeness of the night, and finished his attire by putting on a rabbit-skin cap with hanging lappets which covered the ears, so that no part of him was visible save his mobile and peaky face. "My health is somewhat fragile," he remarked, as he led the way down the passage. "I am compelled to be a valetudinarian."

Our cab was awaiting us outside, and our programmed was evidently prearranged, for the driver started off at once at a rapid pace. Thaddeus Sholto talked incessantly, in a voice which rose high above the rattle of the wheels.

"Bartholomew is a clever fellow," said he. "How do you think he found out where the treasure was? He had come to the conclusion that it was somewhere indoors: so he worked out all the cubic space of the house, and made measurements everywhere, so that not one inch should be unaccounted for. Among other things, he found that the height of the building was seventy-four feet, but on adding together the heights of all the separate rooms, and making every allowance for the space between, which he ascertained by borings, he could not bring the total to more than seventy feet. There were four feet unaccounted for. These could only be at the top of the building. He knocked a hole, therefore, in the lath-and-plaster ceiling of the highest room, and there, sure enough, he came upon another little garret above it, which had been sealed up and was known to no one. In the center stood the treasure-chest, resting upon two rafters. He lowered it through the hole, and there it lies. He computes the value of the jewels at not less than half a million sterling."

At the mention of this gigantic sum we all stared at one another open-eyed. Miss Morstan, could we secure her rights, would change from a needy governess to the richest heiress in England. Surely it was the place of a loyal friend to rejoice at such news; yet I am ashamed to say that selfishness took me by the soul, and that my heart turned as heavy as lead within me. I stammered out some few halting words of congratulation, and then sat downcast, with my head drooped, deaf to the babble of our new acquaintance. He was clearly a confirmed hypochondriac, and I was dreamily conscious that he was pouring forth interminable trains of symptoms, and imploring information as to the composition and action of innumerable quack nostrums, some of which he bore about in a leather case in his pocket. I trust that he may not remember any of the answers which I gave him that night. Holmes declares that he overheard me caution him against the great danger of taking more than two drops of castor oil, while I recommended strychnine in large doses as a sedative. However that may be, I was certainly relieved when our cab pulled up with a jerk and the coachman sprang down to open the door.

"This, Miss Morstan, is Pondicherry Lodge," said Mr. Thaddeus Sholto, as he handed her out.

5 The Tragedy of Pondicherry Lodge

It was nearly eleven o'clock when we reached this final stage of our night's adventures. We had left the damp fog of the great city behind us, and the night was fairly fine. A warm wind blew from the westward, and heavy clouds moved slowly across the sky, with half a moon peeping occasionally through the rifts. It was clear enough to see for some distance, but Thaddeus Sholto took down one of the side-lamps from the carriage to give us a better light upon our way.

Pondicherry Lodge stood in its own grounds, and was girt round with a very high stone wall topped with broken glass. A single narrow iron-clamped door formed the only means of entrance. On this our guide knocked with a peculiar postman-like rat-tat.

"Who is there?" cried a gruff voice from within.

"It is I, McMurdo. You surely know my knock by this time."

There was a grumbling sound and a clanking and jarring of keys. The door swung heavily back, and a short, deep-chested man stood in the opening, with the yellow light of the lantern shining upon his protruded face and twinkling distrustful eyes.

"That you, Mr. Thaddeus? But who are the others? I had no orders about them from the master."

"No, McMurdo? You surprise me! I told my brother last night that I should bring some friends."

"He ain't been out o' his room to-day, Mr. Thaddeus, and I have no orders. You know very well that I must stick to regulations. I can let you in, but your friends must just stop where they are."

This was an unexpected obstacle. Thaddeus Sholto looked about him in a perplexed and helpless manner. "This is too bad of you, McMurdo!" he said. "If I guarantee them, that is enough for you. There is the young lady, too. She cannot wait on the public road at this hour."

"Very sorry, Mr. Thaddeus," said the porter, inexorably. "Folk may be friends o' yours, and yet no friends o' the master's. He pays me well to do my duty, and my duty I'll do. I don't know none o' your friends."

"Oh, yes you do, McMurdo," cried Sherlock Holmes, genially. "I don't think you can have forgotten me. Don't you remember the amateur who fought three rounds with you at Alison's rooms on the night of your benefit four years back?"

"Not Mr. Sherlock Holmes!" roared the prize-fighter. "God's truth! how could I have mistook you? If instead o' standin' there so quiet you had just stepped up and given me that cross-hit of yours under the jaw, I'd ha' known you without a question. Ah, you're one that has wasted your gifts, you have! You might have aimed high, if you had joined the fancy."

"You see, Watson, if all else fails me I have still one of the scientific professions open to me," said Holmes, laughing. "Our friend won't keep us out in the cold now, I am sure."

"In you come, sir, in you come,--you and your friends," he answered. "Very sorry, Mr. Thaddeus, but orders are very strict. Had to be certain of your friends before I let them in."

Inside, a gravel path wound through desolate grounds to a huge clump of a house, square and prosaic, all plunged in shadow save where a moonbeam struck one corner and glimmered in a garret window. The vast size of the building, with its gloom and its deathly silence, struck a chill to the heart. Even Thaddeus Sholto seemed ill at ease, and the lantern quivered and rattled in his hand.

"I cannot understand it," he said. "There must be some mistake. I distinctly told Bartholomew that we should be here, and yet there is no light in his window. I do not know what to make of it."

"Does he always guard the premises in this way?" asked Holmes.

"Yes; he has followed my father's custom. He was the favorite son, you know, and I sometimes think that my father may have told him more than he ever told me. That is Bartholomew's window up there where the moonshine strikes. It is quite bright, but there is no light from within, I think."

"None," said Holmes. "But I see the glint of a light in that little window beside the door."

"Ah, that is the housekeeper's room. That is where old Mrs. Bernstone sits. She can tell us all about it. But perhaps you would not mind waiting here for a minute or two, for if we all go in together and she has no word of our coming she may be alarmed. But hush! what is that?"

He held up the lantern, and his hand shook until the circles of light flickered and wavered all round us. Miss Morstan seized my wrist, and we all stood with thumping hearts, straining our ears. From the great black house there sounded through the silent night the saddest and most pitiful

144

of sounds,--the shrill, broken whimpering of a frightened woman.

"It is Mrs. Bernstone," said Sholto. "She is the only woman in the house. Wait here. I shall be back in a moment." He hurried for the door, and knocked in his peculiar way. We could see a tall old woman admit him, and sway with pleasure at the very sight of him.

"Oh, Mr. Thaddeus, sir, I am so glad you have come! I am so glad you have come, Mr. Thaddeus, sir!" We heard her reiterated rejoicings until the door was closed and her voice died away into a muffled monotone.

Our guide had left us the lantern. Holmes swung it slowly round, and peered keenly at the house, and at the great rubbish-heaps which cumbered the grounds. Miss Morstan and I stood together, and her hand was in mine. A wondrous subtle thing is love, for here were we two who had never seen each other before that day, between whom no word or even look of affection had ever passed, and yet now in an hour of trouble our hands instinctively sought for each other. I have marveled at it since, but at the time it seemed the most natural thing that I should go out to her so, and, as she has often told me, there was in her also the instinct to turn to me for comfort and protection. So we stood hand in hand, like two children, and there was peace in our hearts for all the dark things that surrounded us.

"What a strange place!" she said, looking round.

"It looks as though all the moles in England had been let loose in it. I have seen something of the sort on the side of a hill near Ballarat, where the prospectors had been at work."

"And from the same cause," said Holmes. "These are the traces of the treasure-seekers. You must remember that they were six years looking for it. No wonder that the grounds look like a gravel-pit."

At that moment the door of the house burst open, and Thaddeus Sholto came running out, with his hands thrown forward and terror in his eyes.

"There is something amiss with Bartholomew!" he cried. "I am frightened! My nerves cannot stand it." He was, indeed, half blubbering with fear, and his twitching feeble face peeping out from the great Astrakhan collar had the helpless appealing expression of a terrified child

"Come into the house," said Holmes, in his crisp, firm way.

"Yes, do!" pleaded Thaddeus Sholto. "I really do not feel equal to giving directions."

We all followed him into the housekeeper's room, which stood upon the left-hand side of the passage. The old woman was pacing up and down with a scared look and restless picking fingers, but the sight of Miss Morstan appeared to have a soothing effect upon her.

"God bless your sweet calm face!" she cried, with an hysterical sob. "It does me good to see you. Oh, but I have been sorely tried this day!"

Our companion patted her thin, work-worn hand, and murmured some few words of kindly womanly comfort which brought the color back into the others bloodless cheeks.

"Master has locked himself in and will not answer me," she explained. "All day I have waited to hear from him, for he often likes to be alone; but an hour ago I feared that something was amiss, so I went up and peeped through the key-hole. You must go up, Mr. Thaddeus,—you must go up and look for yourself. I have seen Mr. Bartholomew Sholto in joy and in sorrow for ten long years, but I never saw him with such a face on him as that."

Sherlock Holmes took the lamp and led the way, for Thaddeus Sholto's teeth were chattering in his head. So shaken was he that I had to pass my hand under his arm as we went up the stairs, for his knees were trembling under him. Twice as we ascended Holmes whipped his lens out of his pocket and carefully examined marks which appeared to me to be mere shapeless smudges of dust upon the cocoa-nut matting which served as a stair-carpet. He walked slowly from step to step, holding the lamp, and shooting keen glances to right and left. Miss Morstan had remained behind with the frightened housekeeper.

The third flight of stairs ended in a straight passage of some length, with a great picture in Indian tapestry upon the right of it and three doors upon the left. Holmes advanced along it in the same slow and methodical way, while we kept close at his heels, with our long black shadows streaming backwards down the corridor. The third door was that which we were seeking. Holmes knocked without receiving any answer, and then tried to turn the handle and force it open. It was locked on the inside, however, and by a broad and powerful bolt, as we could see when we set our lamp up against it. The key being turned, however, the hole was not entirely closed. Sherlock Holmes bent down to it, and instantly rose again with a sharp intaking of the breath.

"There is something devilish in this, Watson," said he, more moved than I had ever before seen him. "What do you make of it?"

I stooped to the hole, and recoiled in horror. Moonlight was streaming into the room, and it was bright with a vague and shifty radiance. Looking straight at me, and suspended, as it were, in the air, for all beneath was in shadow, there hung a face,—the very face of our companion Thaddeus. There was the same high, shining head, the same circular bristle of red hair, the same bloodless countenance. The features were set, however, in a horrible smile, a fixed and unnatural grin, which in that still and moonlit room was more jarring to the nerves than any scowl or contortion. So like was the face to that of our little friend that I looked round at him to make sure that he was indeed with us. Then I recalled to mind that he had mentioned to us that his brother and he were twins.

"This is terrible!" I said to Holmes. "What is to be done?"

"The door must come down," he answered, and, springing against it, he put all his weight upon the lock. It creaked and groaned, but did not yield. Together we flung ourselves upon it once more, and this time it gave way with a sudden snap, and we found ourselves within Bartholomew Sholto's chamber.

It appeared to have been fitted up as a chemical laboratory. A double line of glass-stoppered bottles was drawn up upon the wall opposite the door, and the table was littered over with Bunsen burners, test-tubes, and retorts. In the corners stood carboys of acid in wicker baskets. One of these appeared to leak or to have been broken, for a stream of dark-colored liquid had trickled out from it, and the air was heavy with a peculiarly pungent, tar-like odor. A set of steps stood at one side of the room, in the midst of a litter of lath and plaster, and above them there was an opening in the ceiling large enough for a man to pass through. At the foot of the steps a long coil of rope was thrown carelessly together.

By the table, in a wooden arm-chair, the master of the house was seated all in a heap, with his head sunk upon his left shoulder, and that ghastly, inscrutable smile upon his face. He was stiff and cold, and had clearly been dead many hours. It seemed to me that not only his features but all his limbs were twisted and turned in the most fantastic fashion. By his hand upon the table there lay a peculiar instrument,—a brown, close-grained stick, with a stone head like a hammer, rudely lashed on with coarse twine. Beside it was a torn sheet of note-paper with some words scrawled upon it. Holmes glanced at it, and then handed it to me.

"You see," he said, with a significant raising of the eyebrows.

In the light of the lantern I read, with a thrill of horror, "The sign of the four."

"In God's name, what does it all mean?" I asked.

"It means murder," said he, stooping over the dead man. "Ah, I expected it. Look here!" He pointed to what looked like a long, dark thorn stuck in the skin just above the ear.

"It looks like a thorn," said I.

"It is a thorn. You may pick it out. But be careful, for it is poisoned."

I took it up between my finger and thumb. It came away from the skin so readily that hardly any mark was left behind. One tiny speck of blood showed where the puncture had been.

"This is all an insoluble mystery to me," said I. "It grows darker instead of clearer."

"On the contrary," he answered, "it clears every instant. I only require a few missing links to have an entirely connected case."

We had almost forgotten our companion's presence since we entered the chamber. He was still standing in the door-

149

way, the very picture of terror, wringing his hands and moaning to himself. Suddenly, however, he broke out into a sharp, querulous cry.

"The treasure is gone!" he said. "They have robbed him of the treasure! There is the hole through which we lowered it. I helped him to do it! I was the last person who saw him! I left him here last night, and I heard him lock the door as I came down-stairs."

"What time was that?"

"It was ten o'clock. And now he is dead, and the police will be called in, and I shall be suspected of having had a hand in it. Oh, yes, I am sure I shall. But you don't think so, gentlemen? Surely you don't think that it was I? Is it likely that I would have brought you here if it were I? Oh, dear! oh, dear! I know that I shall go mad!" He jerked his arms and stamped his feet in a kind of convulsive frenzy.

"You have no reason for fear, Mr. Sholto," said Holmes, kindly, putting his hand upon his shoulder. "Take my advice, and drive down to the station to report this matter to the police. Offer to assist them in every way. We shall wait here until your return."

The little man obeyed in a half-stupefied fashion, and we heard him stumbling down the stairs in the dark.

6 Sherlock Holmes Gives a Demonstration

"Now, Watson," said Holmes, rubbing his hands, "we have half an hour to ourselves. Let us make good use of it. My case is, as I have told you, almost complete; but we must not err on the side of over-confidence. Simple as the case seems now, there may be something deeper underlying it."

"Simple!" I ejaculated.

"Surely," said he, with something of the air of a clinical professor expounding to his class. "Just sit in the corner there, that your footprints may not complicate matters. Now to work! In the first place, how did these folk come, and how did they go? The door has not been opened since last night. How of the window?" He carried the lamp across to it, muttering his observations aloud the while, but addressing them to himself rather than to me. "Window is snibbed on the inner side. Framework is solid. No hinges at the side. Let us open it. No water-pipe near. Roof quite out of reach. Yet a man has mounted by the window. It rained a little last night. Here is the print of a foot in mould upon the sill. And here is a circular muddy mark, and here again upon the floor, and here again by the table. See here, Watson! This is really a very pretty demonstration."

I looked at the round, well-defined muddy discs. "This is not a footmark," said I.

"It is something much more valuable to us. It is the impression of a wooden stump. You see here on the sill is the boot-mark, a heavy boot with the broad metal heel, and beside it is the mark of the timber-toe."

"It is the wooden-legged man."

"Quite so. But there has been some one else,—a very able and efficient ally. Could you scale that wall, doctor?"

I looked out of the open window. The moon still shone brightly on that angle of the house. We were a good sixty feet from the ground, and, look where I would, I could see no foothold, nor as much as a crevice in the brick-work.

"It is absolutely impossible," I answered.

"Without aid it is so. But suppose you had a friend up here who lowered you this good stout rope which I see in the corner, securing one end of it to this great hook in the wall. Then, I think, if you were an active man, You might swarm up, wooden leg and all. You would depart, of course, in the same fashion, and your ally would draw up the rope, untie it from the hook, shut the window, snib it on the inside, and get away in the way that he originally came. As a minor point it may be noted," he continued, fingering the rope, "that our wooden-legged friend, though a fair climber, was not a professional sailor. His hands were far from horny. My lens discloses more than one blood-mark, especially towards the end of the rope, from which I gather that he slipped down with such velocity that he took the skin off his hand."

"This is all very well," said I, "but the thing becomes more unintelligible than ever. How about this mysterious ally? How came he into the room?"

"Yes, the ally!" repeated Holmes, pensively. "There are features of interest about this ally. He lifts the case from the regions of the commonplace. I fancy that this ally breaks fresh ground in the annals of crime in this country,—though parallel cases suggest themselves from India, and, if my memory serves me, from Senegambia."

"How came he, then?" I reiterated. "The door is locked, the window is inaccessible. Was it through the chimney?"

"The grate is much too small," he answered. "I had already considered that possibility."

"How then?" I persisted.

"You will not apply my precept," he said, shaking his head. "How often have I said to you that when you have eliminated the impossible whatever remains, HOWEVER IMPROBABLE, must be the truth? We know that he did not come through the door, the window, or the chimney. We also know that he could not have been concealed in the room, as there is no concealment possible. Whence, then, did he come?"

"He came through the hole in the roof," I cried.

"Of course he did. He must have done so. If you will have the kindness to hold the lamp for me, we shall now extend our researches to the room above,—the secret room in which the treasure was found."

He mounted the steps, and, seizing a rafter with either hand, he swung himself up into the garret. Then, lying on his face, he reached down for the lamp and held it while I followed him.

The chamber in which we found ourselves was about ten feet one way and six the other. The floor was formed by the rafters, with thin lath-and-plaster between, so that in walking one had to step from beam to beam. The roof ran up to an apex, and was evidently the inner shell of the true roof of the house. There was no furniture of any sort, and the accumulated dust of years lay thick upon the floor.

"Here you are, you see," said Sherlock Holmes, putting his hand against the sloping wall. "This is a trap-door which leads out on to the roof. I can press it back, and here is the roof itself, sloping at a gentle angle. This, then, is the way by which Number One entered. Let us see if we can find any other traces of his individuality."

He held down the lamp to the floor, and as he did so I saw for the second time that night a startled, surprised look come over his face. For myself, as I followed his gaze my skin was cold under my clothes. The floor was covered thickly with the prints of a naked foot,—clear, well defined, perfectly formed, but scarce half the size of those of an ordinary man.

"Holmes," I said, in a whisper, "a child has done the horrid thing."

He had recovered his self-possession in an instant. "I was staggered for the moment," he said, "but the thing is quite natural. My memory failed me, or I should have been able to foretell it. There is nothing more to be learned here. Let us go down."

"What is your theory, then, as to those footmarks?" I asked, eagerly, when we had regained the lower room once more.

"My dear Watson, try a little analysis yourself," said he, with a touch of impatience. "You know my methods. Apply them, and it will be instructive to compare results."

"I cannot conceive anything which will cover the facts," I answered.

"It will be clear enough to you soon," he said, in an off-hand way. "I think that there is nothing else of importance here, but I will look." He whipped out his lens and a tape measure, and hurried about the room on his knees, measuring, comparing, examining, with his long thin nose only a few inches from the planks, and his beady eyes gleaming and deep-set like those of a bird. So swift, silent, and furtive were his movements, like those of a trained blood-hound picking out a scent, that I could not but think what a terrible criminal he would have made had he turned his energy and sagacity against the law, instead of exerting them in its defense. As he hunted about, he kept muttering to himself, and finally he broke out into a loud crow of delight.

"We are certainly in luck," said he. "We ought to have very little trouble now. Number One has had the misfortune to tread in the creosote. You can see the outline of the edge of his small foot here at the side of this evil-smelling mess. The carboy has been cracked, You see, and the stuff has leaked out."

"What then?" I asked.

"Why, we have got him, that's all," said he. "I know a dog that would follow that scent to the world's end. If a pack can track a trailed herring across a shire, how far can a specially-trained hound follow so pungent a smell as this? It sounds like a sum in the rule of three. The answer should give us the— But halloo! here are the accredited representatives of the law."

Heavy steps and the clamor of loud voices were audible from below, and the hall door shut with a loud crash.

"Before they come," said Holmes, "just put your hand here on this poor fellow's arm, and here on his leg. What do you feel?"

"The muscles are as hard as a board," I answered.

"Quite so. They are in a state of extreme contraction, far exceeding the usual rigor mortis. Coupled with this distortion of the face, this Hippocratic smile, or 'risus sardonicus,' as the old writers called it, what conclusion would it suggest to your mind?"

"Death from some powerful vegetable alkaloid," I answered,—"some strychnine-like substance which would produce tetanus."

"That was the idea which occurred to me the instant I saw the drawn muscles of the face. On getting into the room I at once looked for the means by which the poison had entered the system. As you saw, I discovered a thorn which had been driven or shot with no great force into the scalp. You observe that the part struck was that which would be turned towards the hole in the ceiling if the man were erect in his chair. Now examine the thorn."

I took it up gingerly and held it in the light of the lantern. It was long, sharp, and black, with a glazed look near the point as though some gummy substance had dried upon it. The blunt end had been trimmed and rounded off with a knife.

"Is that an English thorn?" he asked.

"No, it certainly is not."

"With all these data you should be able to draw some just inference. But here are the regulars: so the auxiliary forces may beat a retreat."

As he spoke, the steps which had been coming nearer sounded loudly on the passage, and a very stout, portly man in a gray suit strode heavily into the room. He was red-faced, burly and plethoric, with a pair of very small twinkling eyes which looked keenly out from between swollen and puffy pouches. He was closely followed by an inspector in uniform, and by the still palpitating Thaddeus Sholto.

"Here's a business!" he cried, in a muffled, husky voice.

"Here's a pretty business! But who are all these? Why, the house seems to be as full as a rabbit-warren!"

"I think you must recollect me, Mr. Athelney Jones," said Holmes, quietly.

"Why, of course I do!" he wheezed. "It's Mr. Sherlock Holmes, the theorist. Remember you! I'll never forget how you lectured us all on causes and inferences and effects in the Bishopgate jewel case. It's true you set us on the right track; but you'll own now that it was more by good luck than good guidance."

"It was a piece of very simple reasoning."

"Oh, come, now, come! Never be ashamed to own up. But what is all this? Bad business! Bad business! Stern facts here,—no room for theories. How lucky that I happened to be out at Norwood over another case! I was at the station when the message arrived. What d'you think the man died of?"

"Oh, this is hardly a case for me to theorize over," said Holmes, dryly.

"No, no. Still, we can't deny that you hit the nail on the head sometimes. Dear me! Door locked, I understand. Jewels worth half a million missing. How was the window?"

"Fastened; but there are steps on the sill."

"Well, well, if it was fastened the steps could have nothing to do with the matter. That's common sense. Man might have died in a fit; but then the jewels are missing. Ha! I have a theory. These flashes come upon me at times.—Just step outside, sergeant, and you, Mr. Sholto. Your friend can remain.—What do you think of this, Holmes? Sholto was, on his own confession, with his brother last night. The brother died in a fit, on which Sholto walked off with the treasure. How's that?"

"On which the dead man very considerately got up and locked the door on the inside."

"Hum! There's a flaw there. Let us apply common sense to the matter. This Thaddeus Sholto WAS with his brother; there WAS a quarrel; so much we know. The brother is dead and the jewels are gone. So much also we know. No one saw the brother from the time Thaddeus left him. His bed had not been slept in. Thaddeus is evidently in a most disturbed state of mind. His appearance is—well, not attractive. You see that I am weaving my web round Thaddeus. The net begins to close upon him."

"You are not quite in possession of the facts yet," said Holmes. "This splinter of wood, which I have every reason to believe to be poisoned, was in the man's scalp where you still see the mark; this card, inscribed as you see it, was on the table; and beside it lay this rather curious stone-headed instrument. How does all that fit into your theory?"

"Confirms it in every respect," said the fat detective, pompously. "House is full of Indian curiosities. Thaddeus brought this up, and if this splinter be poisonous Thaddeus may as well have made murderous use of it as any other man. The card is some hocus-pocus,—a blind, as like as not. The only question is, how did he depart? Ah, of course, here is a hole in the roof." With great activity, considering his bulk, he sprang up the steps and squeezed through into the garret, and immediately afterwards we heard his exulting voice proclaiming that he had found the trap-door.

"He can find something," remarked Holmes, shrugging his shoulders. "He has occasional glimmerings of reason. *Il n'y a pas des sots si incommodes que ceux qui ont de l'esprit!*"

"You see!" said Athelney Jones, reappearing down the steps again. "Facts are better than mere theories, after all. My view of the case is confirmed. There is a trap-door communicating with the roof, and it is partly open."

"It was I who opened it."

"Oh, indeed! You did notice it, then?" He seemed a little crestfallen at the discovery. "Well, whoever noticed it, it shows how our gentleman got away. Inspector!"

"Yes, sir," from the passage.

"Ask Mr. Sholto to step this way.—Mr. Sholto, it is my duty to inform you that anything which you may say will be used against you. I arrest you in the queen's name as being concerned in the death of your brother."

"There, now! Didn't I tell you!" cried the poor little man, throwing out his hands, and looking from one to the other of us.

"Don't trouble yourself about it, Mr. Sholto," said Holmes. "I think that I can engage to clear you of the charge."

"Don't promise too much, Mr. Theorist,—don't promise too much!" snapped the detective. "You may find it a harder matter than you think."

"Not only will I clear him, Mr. Jones, but I will make you a free present of the name and description of one of the two people who were in this room last night. His name, I have every reason to believe, is Jonathan Small. He is a poorly-educated man, small, active, with his right leg off, and wearing a wooden stump which is worn away upon the inner side. His left boot has a coarse, square-toed sole, with an iron band round the heel. He is a middle-aged man, much sunburned, and has been a convict. These few indications may be of some assistance to you, coupled with the fact that there is a good deal of skin missing from the palm of his hand. The other man—"

"Ah! the other man—?" asked Athelney Jones, in a sneering voice, but impressed none the less, as I could easily see, by the precision of the other's manner.

"Is a rather curious person," said Sherlock Holmes, turning upon his heel. "I hope before very long to be able to introduce you to the pair of them.—A word with you, Watson."

He led me out to the head of the stair. "This unexpected occurrence," he said, "has caused us rather to lose sight of the original purpose of our journey."

"I have just been thinking so," I answered. "It is not right that Miss Morstan should remain in this stricken house."

"No. You must escort her home. She lives with Mrs. Cecil Forrester, in Lower Camberwell: so it is not very far. I will wait for you here if you will drive out again. Or perhaps you are too tired?"

"By no means. I don't think I could rest until I know more of this fantastic business. I have seen something of the rough side of life, but I give you my word that this quick succession of strange surprises to-night has shaken my nerve completely. I should like, however, to see the matter through with you, now that I have got so far."

"Your presence will be of great service to me," he answered. "We shall work the case out independently, and leave this fellow Jones to exult over any mare's-nest which he may choose to construct. When you have dropped Miss Morstan I wish you to go on to No. 3 Pinchin Lane, down near the water's edge at Lambeth. The third house on the right-hand side is a bird-stuffer's: Sherman is the name. You will see a weasel holding a young rabbit in the window. Knock old Sherman up, and tell him, with my compliments, that I want Toby at once. You will bring Toby back in the cab with you."

"A dog, I suppose."

"Yes,—a queer mongrel, with a most amazing power of scent. I would rather have Toby's help than that of the whole detective force of London."

"I shall bring him, then," said I. "It is one now. I ought to be back before three, if I can get a fresh horse."

"And I," said Holmes, "shall see what I can learn from Mrs. Bernstone, and from the Indian servant, who, Mr. Thaddeus tell me, sleeps in the next garret. Then I shall study the great Jones's methods and listen to his not too delicate sarcasms. '*Wir sind gewohnt das die Menschen verhoehnen was sie nicht verstehen.*' Goethe is always pithy."

7 The Episode of the Barrel

The police had brought a cab with them, and in this I escorted
Miss Morstan back to her home. After the angelic fashion of
women, she had borne trouble with a calm face as long as
there was some one weaker than herself to support, and I had
found her bright and placid by the side of the frightened
housekeeper. In the cab, however, she first turned faint, and
then burst into a passion of weeping,—so sorely had she been
tried by the adventures of the night. She has told me since
that she thought me cold and distant upon that journey. She
little guessed the struggle within my breast, or the effort of
self-restraint which held me back. My sympathies and my love
went out to her, even as my hand had in the garden. I felt that
years of the conventionalities of life could not teach me to
know her sweet, brave nature as had this one day of strange
experiences. Yet there were two thoughts which sealed the
words of affection upon my lips. She was weak and helpless,
shaken in mind and nerve. It was to take her at a
disadvantage to obtrude love upon her at such a time. Worse
still, she was rich. If Holmes's researches were successful, she
would be an heiress. Was it fair, was it honorable, that a half-
pay surgeon should take such advantage of an intimacy which
chance had brought about? Might she not look upon me as a
mere vulgar fortune-seeker? I could not bear to risk that such
a thought should cross her mind. This Agra treasure
intervened like an impassable barrier between us.

It was nearly two o'clock when we reached Mrs. Cecil
Forrester's. The servants had retired hours ago, but Mrs.

Forrester had been so interested by the strange message which Miss Morstan had received that she had sat up in the hope of her return. She opened the door herself, a middle-aged, graceful woman, and it gave me joy to see how tenderly her arm stole round the other's waist and how motherly was the voice in which she greeted her. She was clearly no mere paid dependant, but an honored friend. I was introduced, and Mrs. Forrester earnestly begged me to step in and tell her our adventures. I explained, however, the importance of my errand, and promised faithfully to call and report any progress which we might make with the case. As we drove away I stole a glance back, and I still seem to see that little group on the step, the two graceful, clinging figures, the half-opened door, the hall light shining through stained glass, the barometer, and the bright stair-rods. It was soothing to catch even that passing glimpse of a tranquil English home in the midst of the wild, dark business which had absorbed us.

And the more I thought of what had happened, the wilder and darker it grew. I reviewed the whole extraordinary sequence of events as I rattled on through the silent gas-lit streets. There was the original problem: that at least was pretty clear now. The death of Captain Morstan, the sending of the pearls, the advertisement, the letter,—we had had light upon all those events. They had only led us, however, to a deeper and far more tragic mystery. The Indian treasure, the curious plan found among Morstan's baggage, the strange scene at Major Sholto's death, the rediscovery of the treasure immediately followed by the murder of the discoverer, the very singular accompaniments to the crime, the footsteps, the remarkable weapons, the words upon the card, corresponding with those upon Captain Morstan's chart,—here was indeed a labyrinth in which a man less singularly endowed than my fellow-lodger might well despair of ever finding the clue.

Pinchin Lane was a row of shabby two-storied brick houses in the lower quarter of Lambeth. I had to knock for some time at No. 3 before I could make my impression. At last, however, there was the glint of a candle behind the blind, and a face looked out at the upper window.

"Go on, you drunken vagabond," said the face. "If you kick up any more row I'll open the kennels and let out forty-three dogs upon you."

"If you'll let one out it's just what I have come for," said I.

"Go on!" yelled the voice. "So help me gracious, I have a wiper in the bag, an' I'll drop it on your 'ead if you don't hook it."

"But I want a dog," I cried.

"I won't be argued with!" shouted Mr. Sherman. "Now stand clear, for when I say 'three,' down goes the wiper."

"Mr. Sherlock Holmes—" I began, but the words had a most magical effect, for the window instantly slammed down, and within a minute the door was unbarred and open. Mr. Sherman was a lanky, lean old man, with stooping shoulders, a stringy neck, and blue-tinted glasses.

"A friend of Mr. Sherlock is always welcome," said he. "Step in, sir. Keep clear of the badger; for he bites. Ah, naughty, naughty, would you take a nip at the gentleman?" This to a stoat which thrust its wicked head and red eyes between the bars of its cage. "Don't mind that, sir: it's only a slow-worm. It hain't got no fangs, so I gives it the run o' the room, for it keeps the beetles down. You must not mind my bein' just a little short wi' you at first, for I'm guyed at by the children, and there's many a one just comes down this lane to knock me up. What was it that Mr. Sherlock Holmes wanted, sir?"

"He wanted a dog of yours."

"Ah! that would be Toby."

"Yes, Toby was the name."

"Toby lives at No. 7 on the left here." He moved slowly forward with his candle among the queer animal family which he had gathered round him. In the uncertain, shadowy light I could see dimly that there were glancing, glimmering eyes peeping down at us from every cranny and corner. Even the rafters above our heads were lined by solemn fowls, who lazily shifted their weight from one leg to the other as our voices disturbed their slumbers.

Toby proved to be an ugly, long-haired, lop-eared creature, half spaniel and half lurcher, brown-and-white in color, with a very clumsy waddling gait. It accepted after some hesitation a lump of sugar which the old naturalist handed to me, and, having thus sealed an alliance, it followed me to the cab, and made no difficulties about accompanying me. It had just struck three on the Palace clock when I found myself back once more at Pondicherry Lodge. The ex-prize-fighter McMurdo had, I found, been arrested as an accessory, and both he and Mr. Sholto had been marched off to the station. Two constables guarded the narrow gate, but they allowed me to pass with the dog on my mentioning the detective's name.

Holmes was standing on the door-step, with his hands in his pockets, smoking his pipe.

"Ah, you have him there!" said he. "Good dog, then! Athenley Jones has gone. We have had an immense display of energy since you left. He has arrested not only friend Thaddeus, but the gatekeeper, the housekeeper, and the Indian servant. We have the place to ourselves, but for a sergeant up-stairs. Leave the dog here, and come up."

We tied Toby to the hall table, and reascended the stairs. The room was as he had left it, save that a sheet had been draped over the central figure. A weary-looking police-sergeant reclined in the corner.

"Lend me your bull's-eye, sergeant," said my companion. "Now tie this bit of card round my neck, so as to hang it in front of me. Thank you. Now I must kick off my boots and stockings.—Just you carry them down with you, Watson. I am going to do a little climbing. And dip my handkerchief into the creosote. That will do. Now come up into the garret with me for a moment."

We clambered up through the hole. Holmes turned his light once more upon the footsteps in the dust.

"I wish you particularly to notice these footmarks," he said. "Do you observe anything noteworthy about them?"

"They belong," I said, "to a child or a small woman."

"Apart from their size, though. Is there nothing else?"

"They appear to be much as other footmarks."

"Not at all. Look here! This is the print of a right foot in the dust. Now I make one with my naked foot beside it. What is the chief difference?"

"Your toes are all cramped together. The other print has each toe distinctly divided."

"Quite so. That is the point. Bear that in mind. Now, would you kindly step over to that flap-window and smell the edge of the wood-work? I shall stay here, as I have this handkerchief in my hand."

I did as he directed, and was instantly conscious of a strong tarry smell.

"That is where he put his foot in getting out. If YOU can trace him, I should think that Toby will have no difficulty. Now run down-stairs, loose the dog, and look out for Blondin."

By the time that I got out into the grounds Sherlock Holmes was on the roof, and I could see him like an enormous glow-worm crawling very slowly along the ridge. I lost sight of him behind a stack of chimneys, but he presently reappeared, and then vanished once more upon the opposite side. When I made my way round there I found him seated at one of the corner eaves.

"That you, Watson?" he cried.

"Yes."

"This is the place. What is that black thing down there?"

"A water-barrel."

"Top on it?"

"Yes."

"No sign of a ladder?"

"No."

"Confound the fellow! It's a most break-neck place. I ought to be able to come down where he could climb up. The water-pipe feels pretty firm. Here goes, anyhow."

There was a scuffling of feet, and the lantern began to come steadily down the side of the wall. Then with a light spring he came on to the barrel, and from there to the earth.

"It was easy to follow him," he said, drawing on his

stockings and boots. "Tiles were loosened the whole way along, and in his hurry he had dropped this. It confirms my diagnosis, as you doctors express it."

The object which he held up to me was a small pocket or pouch woven out of colored grasses and with a few tawdry beads strung round it. In shape and size it was not unlike a cigarette-case. Inside were half a dozen spines of dark wood, sharp at one end and rounded at the other, like that which had struck Bartholomew Sholto.

"They are hellish things," said he. "Look out that you don't prick yourself. I'm delighted to have them, for the chances are that they are all he has. There is the less fear of you or me finding one in our skin before long. I would sooner face a Martini bullet, myself. Are you game for a six-mile trudge, Watson?"

"Certainly," I answered.

"Your leg will stand it?"

"Oh, yes."

"Here you are, doggy! Good old Toby! Smell it, Toby, smell it!" He pushed the creosote handkerchief under the dog's nose, while the creature stood with its fluffy legs separated, and with a most comical cock to its head, like a connoisseur sniffing the bouquet of a famous vintage. Holmes then threw the handkerchief to a distance, fastened a stout cord to the mongrel's collar, and led him to the foot of the water-barrel. The creature instantly broke into a succession of high, tremulous yelps, and, with his nose on the ground, and his tail in the air, pattered off upon the trail at a pace which strained his leash and kept us at the top of our speed.

The east had been gradually whitening, and we could now see some distance in the cold gray light. The square, massive house, with its black, empty windows and high, bare walls, towered up, sad and forlorn, behind us. Our course led right across the grounds, in and out among the trenches and pits with which they were scarred and intersected. The whole place, with its scattered dirt-heaps and ill-grown shrubs, had a blighted, ill-omened look which harmonized with the black tragedy which hung over it.

On reaching the boundary wall Toby ran along, whining eagerly, underneath its shadow, and stopped finally in a corner screened by a young beech. Where the two walls joined, several bricks had been loosened, and the crevices left were worn down and rounded upon the lower side, as though they had frequently been used as a ladder. Holmes clambered up, and, taking the dog from me, he dropped it over upon the other side.

"There's the print of wooden-leg's hand," he remarked, as I mounted up beside him. "You see the slight smudge of blood upon the white plaster. What a lucky thing it is that we have had no very heavy rain since yesterday! The scent will lie upon the road in spite of their eight-and-twenty hours' start."

I confess that I had my doubts myself when I reflected upon the great traffic which had passed along the London road in the interval. My fears were soon appeased, however. Toby never hesitated or swerved, but waddled on in his peculiar rolling fashion. Clearly, the pungent smell of the creosote rose high above all other contending scents.

"Do not imagine," said Holmes, "that I depend for my success in this case upon the mere chance of one of these fellows having put his foot in the chemical. I have knowledge now which would enable me to trace them in many different ways. This, however, is the readiest and, since fortune has put it into our hands, I should be culpable if I neglected it. It has, however, prevented the case from becoming the pretty little intellectual problem which it at one time promised to be. There might have been some credit to be gained out of it, but for this too palpable clue."

"There is credit, and to spare," said I. "I assure you, Holmes, that I marvel at the means by which you obtain your results in this case, even more than I did in the Jefferson Hope Murder. The thing seems to me to be deeper and more inexplicable. How, for example, could you describe with such confidence the wooden-legged man?"

"Pshaw, my dear boy! it was simplicity itself. I don't wish to be theatrical. It is all patent and above-board. Two officers who are in command of a convict-guard learn an important secret as to buried treasure. A map is drawn for them by an Englishman named Jonathan Small. You remember that we saw the name upon the chart in Captain Morstan's possession. He had signed it in behalf of himself and his associates,—the sign of the four, as he somewhat dramatically called it. Aided by this chart, the officers—or one of them—gets the treasure and brings it to England, leaving, we will suppose, some condition under which he received it unfulfilled. Now, then, why did not Jonathan Small get the treasure himself? The answer is obvious. The chart is dated at a time when Morstan was brought into close association with convicts. Jonathan Small did not get the treasure because he and his associates were themselves convicts and could not get away."

"But that is mere speculation," said I.

"It is more than that. It is the only hypothesis which covers the facts. Let us see how it fits in with the sequel. Major Sholto remains at peace for some years, happy in the possession of his treasure. Then he receives a letter from India which gives him a great fright. What was that?"

"A letter to say that the men whom he had wronged had been set free."

"Or had escaped. That is much more likely, for he would have known what their term of imprisonment was. It would not have been a surprise to him. What does he do then? He guards himself against a wooden-legged man,—a white man, mark you, for he mistakes a white tradesman for him, and actually fires a pistol at him. Now, only one white man's name is on the chart. The others are Hindus or Mohammedans. There is no other white man. Therefore we may say with confidence that the wooden-legged man is identical with Jonathan Small. Does the reasoning strike you as being faulty?"

"No: it is clear and concise."

"Well, now, let us put ourselves in the place of Jonathan Small. Let us look at it from his point of view. He comes to England with the double idea of regaining what he would consider to be his rights and of having his revenge upon the man who had wronged him. He found out where Sholto lived, and very possibly he established communications with some one inside the house. There is this butler, Lal Rao, whom we have not seen. Mrs. Bernstone gives him far from a good character. Small could not find out, however, where the treasure was hid, for no one ever knew, save the major and one faithful servant who had died. Suddenly Small learns that the major is on his death-bed. In a frenzy lest the secret of the treasure die with him, he runs the gauntlet of the guards, makes his way to the dying man's window, and is only deterred from entering by the presence of his two sons. Mad with hate, however, against the dead man, he enters the room that night, searches his private papers in the hope of discovering some memorandum relating to the treasure, and finally leaves a memento of his visit in the short inscription upon the card. He had doubtless planned beforehand that should he slay the major he would leave some such record upon the body as a sign that it was not a common murder, but, from the point of view of the four associates, something in the nature of an act of justice. Whimsical and bizarre conceits of this kind are common enough in the annals of crime, and usually afford valuable indications as to the criminal. Do you follow all this?"

"Very clearly."

"Now, what could Jonathan Small do? He could only continue to keep a secret watch upon the efforts made to find the treasure. Possibly he leaves England and only comes back at intervals. Then comes the discovery of the garret, and he is instantly informed of it. We again trace the presence of some confederate in the household. Jonathan, with his wooden leg, is utterly unable to reach the lofty room of Bartholomew Sholto. He takes with him, however, a rather curious associate, who gets over this difficulty, but dips his naked foot into creosote, whence comes Toby, and a six-mile limp for a half-pay officer with a damaged tendon Achilles."

"But it was the associate, and not Jonathan, who committed the crime."

"Quite so. And rather to Jonathan's disgust, to judge by the way he stamped about when he got into the room. He bore no grudge against Bartholomew Sholto, and would have preferred if he could have been simply bound and gagged. He did not wish to put his head in a halter. There was no help for it, however: the savage instincts of his companion had broken out, and the poison had done its work: so Jonathan Small left his record, lowered the treasure-box to the ground, and followed it himself. That was the train of events as far as I can decipher them. Of course as to his personal appearance he must be middle-aged, and must be sunburned after serving his time in such an oven as the Andamans. His height is readily calculated from the length of his stride, and we know that he was bearded. His hairiness was the one point which impressed itself upon Thaddeus Sholto when he saw him at the window. I don't know that there is anything else."

"The associate?"

"Ah, well, there is no great mystery in that. But you will know all about it soon enough. How sweet the morning air is! See how that one little cloud floats like a pink feather from some gigantic flamingo. Now the red rim of the sun pushes itself over the London cloud-bank. It shines on a good many folk, but on none, I dare bet, who are on a stranger errand than you and I. How small we feel with our petty ambitions and strivings in the presence of the great elemental forces of nature! Are you well up in your Jean Paul?"

"Fairly so. I worked back to him through Carlyle."

"That was like following the brook to the parent lake. He makes one curious but profound remark. It is that the chief proof of man's real greatness lies in his perception of his own smallness. It argues, you see, a power of comparison and of appreciation which is in itself a proof of nobility. There is much food for thought in Richter. You have not a pistol, have you?"

"I have my stick."

"It is just possible that we may need something of the sort if we get to their lair. Jonathan I shall leave to you, but if the other turns nasty I shall shoot him dead." He took out his revolver as he spoke, and, having loaded two of the chambers, he put it back into the right-hand pocket of his jacket.

We had during this time been following the guidance of Toby down the half-rural villa-lined roads which lead to the metropolis. Now, however, we were beginning to come among continuous streets, where laborers and dockmen were already astir, and slatternly women were taking down shutters and brushing door-steps. At the square-topped corner public houses business was just beginning, and rough-looking men were emerging, rubbing their sleeves across their beards after their morning wet. Strange dogs sauntered up and stared wonderingly at us as we passed, but our inimitable Toby looked neither to the right nor to the left, but trotted onwards with his nose to the ground and an occasional eager whine which spoke of a hot scent.

We had traversed Streatham, Brixton, Camberwell, and now found ourselves in Kennington Lane, having borne away through the side-streets to the east of the Oval. The men whom we pursued seemed to have taken a curiously zigzag road, with the idea probably of escaping observation. They had never kept to the main road if a parallel side-street would serve their turn. At the foot of Kennington Lane they had edged away to the left through Bond Street and Miles Street. Where the latter street turns into Knight's Place, Toby ceased to advance, but began to run backwards and forwards with one ear cocked and the other drooping, the very picture of canine indecision. Then he waddled round in circles, looking up to us from time to time, as if to ask for sympathy in his embarrassment.

"What the deuce is the matter with the dog?" growled Holmes. "They surely would not take a cab, or go off in a balloon."

"Perhaps they stood here for some time," I suggested.

"Ah! it's all right. He's off again," said my companion, in a tone of relief.

He was indeed off, for after sniffing round again he suddenly made up his mind, and darted away with an energy and determination such as he had not yet shown. The scent appeared to be much hotter than before, for he had not even to put his nose on the ground, but tugged at his leash and tried to break into a run. I cold see by the gleam in Holmes's eyes that he thought we were nearing the end of our journey.

Our course now ran down Nine Elms until we came to Broderick and Nelson's large timber-yard, just past the White Eagle tavern. Here the dog, frantic with excitement, turned down through the side-gate into the enclosure, where the sawyers were already at work. On the dog raced through sawdust and shavings, down an alley, round a passage, between two wood-piles, and finally, with a triumphant yelp, sprang upon a large barrel which still stood upon the hand-trolley on which it had been brought. With lolling tongue and blinking eyes, Toby stood upon the cask, looking from one to the other of us for some sign of appreciation. The staves of the barrel and the wheels of the trolley were smeared with a dark liquid, and the whole air was heavy with the smell of creosote.

Sherlock Holmes and I looked blankly at each other, and then burst simultaneously into an uncontrollable fit of laughter.

8 The Baker Street Irregulars

"What now?" I asked. "Toby has lost his character for infallibility."

"He acted according to his lights," said Holmes, lifting him down from the barrel and walking him out of the timber-yard. "If you consider how much creosote is carted about London in one day, it is no great wonder that our trail should have been crossed. It is much used now, especially for the seasoning of wood. Poor Toby is not to blame."

"We must get on the main scent again, I suppose."

"Yes. And, fortunately, we have no distance to go. Evidently what puzzled the dog at the corner of Knight's Place was that there were two different trails running in opposite directions. We took the wrong one. It only remains to follow the other."

There was no difficulty about this. On leading Toby to the place where he had committed his fault, he cast about in a wide circle and finally dashed off in a fresh direction.

"We must take care that he does not now bring us to the place where the creosote-barrel came from," I observed.

"I had thought of that. But you notice that he keeps on the pavement, whereas the barrel passed down the roadway. No, we are on the true scent now."

It tended down towards the river-side, running through Belmont Place and Prince's Street. At the end of Broad Street it ran right down to the water's edge, where there was a small wooden wharf. Toby led us to the very edge of this, and there stood whining, looking out on the dark current beyond.

"We are out of luck," said Holmes. "They have taken to a boat here." Several small punts and skiffs were lying about in the water and on the edge of the wharf. We took Toby round to each in turn, but, though he sniffed earnestly, he made no sign.

Close to the rude landing-stage was a small brick house, with a wooden placard slung out through the second window. "Mordecai Smith" was printed across it in large letters, and, underneath, "Boats to hire by the hour or day." A second inscription above the door informed us that a steam launch was kept,—a statement which was confirmed by a great pile of coke upon the jetty. Sherlock Holmes looked slowly round, and his face assumed an ominous expression.

"This looks bad," said he. "These fellows are sharper than I expected. They seem to have covered their tracks. There has, I fear, been preconcerted management here."

He was approaching the door of the house, when it opened, and a little, curly-headed lad of six came running out, followed by a stoutish, red-faced woman with a large sponge in her hand.

"You come back and be washed, Jack," she shouted. "Come back, you young imp; for if your father comes home and finds you like that, he'll let us hear of it."

"Dear little chap!" said Holmes, strategically. "What a rosy-cheeked young rascal! Now, Jack, is there anything you would like?"

The youth pondered for a moment. "I'd like a shillin'," said he.

"Nothing you would like better?"

"I'd like two shillin' better," the prodigy answered, after some thought.

"Here you are, then! Catch!—A fine child, Mrs. Smith!"

"Lor' bless you, sir, he is that, and forward. He gets a'most too much for me to manage, 'specially when my man is away days at a time."

"Away, is he?" said Holmes, in a disappointed voice. "I am sorry for that, for I wanted to speak to Mr. Smith."

"He's been away since yesterday mornin', sir, and, truth to tell, I am beginnin' to feel frightened about him. But if it was about a boat, sir, maybe I could serve as well."

"I wanted to hire his steam launch."

"Why, bless you, sir, it is in the steam launch that he has gone. That's what puzzles me; for I know there ain't more coals in her than would take her to about Woolwich and back. If he'd been away in the barge I'd ha' thought nothin'; for many a time a job has taken him as far as Gravesend, and then if there was much doin' there he might ha' stayed over. But what good is a steam launch without coals?"

"He might have bought some at a wharf down the river."

"He might, sir, but it weren't his way. Many a time I've heard him call out at the prices they charge for a few odd bags. Besides, I don't like that wooden-legged man, wi' his ugly face and outlandish talk. What did he want always knockin' about here for?"

"A wooden-legged man?" said Holmes, with bland surprise.

"Yes, sir, a brown, monkey-faced chap that's called

more'n once for my old man. It was him that roused him up yesternight, and, what's more, my man knew he was comin', for he had steam up in the launch. I tell you straight, sir, I don't feel easy in my mind about it."

"But, my dear Mrs. Smith," said Holmes, shrugging his shoulders, "You are frightening yourself about nothing. How could you possibly tell that it was the wooden-legged man who came in the night? I don't quite understand how you can be so sure."

"His voice, sir. I knew his voice, which is kind o' thick and foggy. He tapped at the winder,—about three it would be. 'Show a leg, matey,' says he: 'time to turn out guard.' My old man woke up Jim,—that's my eldest,—and away they went, without so much as a word to me. I could hear the wooden leg clackin' on the stones."

"And was this wooden-legged man alone?"

"Couldn't say, I am sure, sir. I didn't hear no one else."

"I am sorry, Mrs. Smith, for I wanted a steam launch, and I have heard good reports of the—Let me see, what is her name?"

"The Aurora, sir."

"Ah! She's not that old green launch with a yellow line, very broad in the beam?"

"No, indeed. She's as trim a little thing as any on the river. She's been fresh painted, black with two red streaks."

"Thanks. I hope that you will hear soon from Mr. Smith. I am going down the river; and if I should see anything of the Aurora I shall let him know that you are uneasy. A black funnel, you say?"

"No, sir. Black with a white band."

"Ah, of course. It was the sides which were black. Good-morning, Mrs. Smith.—There is a boatman here with a wherry, Watson. We shall take it and cross the river.

"The main thing with people of that sort," said Holmes, as we sat in the sheets of the wherry, "is never to let them think that their information can be of the slightest importance to you. If you do, they will instantly shut up like an oyster. If you listen to them under protest, as it were, you are very likely to get what you want."

"Our course now seems pretty clear," said I.

"What would you do, then?"

"I would engage a launch and go down the river on the track of the Aurora."

"My dear fellow, it would be a colossal task. She may have touched at any wharf on either side of the stream between here and Greenwich. Below the bridge there is a perfect labyrinth of landing-places for miles. It would take you days and days to exhaust them, if you set about it alone."

"Employ the police, then."

"No. I shall probably call Athelney Jones in at the last moment. He is not a bad fellow, and I should not like to do anything which would injure him professionally. But I have a fancy for working it out myself, now that we have gone so far."

"Could we advertise, then, asking for information from wharfingers?"

"Worse and worse! Our men would know that the chase was hot at their heels, and they would be off out of the country. As it is, they are likely enough to leave, but as long as they think they are perfectly safe they will be in no hurry.

Jones's energy will be of use to us there, for his view of the case is sure to push itself into the daily press, and the runaways will think that every one is off on the wrong scent."

"What are we to do, then?" I asked, as we landed near Millbank Penitentiary.

"Take this hansom, drive home, have some breakfast, and get an hour's sleep. It is quite on the cards that we may be afoot to-night again. Stop at a telegraph-office, cabby! We will keep Toby, for he may be of use to us yet."

We pulled up at the Great Peter Street post-office, and Holmes dispatched his wire. "Whom do you think that is to?" he asked, as we resumed our journey.

"I am sure I don't know."

"You remember the Baker Street division of the detective police force whom I employed in the Jefferson Hope case?"

"Well," said I, laughing.

"This is just the case where they might be invaluable. If they fail, I have other resources; but I shall try them first. That wire was to my dirty little lieutenant, Wiggins, and I expect that he and his gang will be with us before we have finished our breakfast."

It was between eight and nine o'clock now, and I was conscious of a strong reaction after the successive excitements of the night. I was limp and weary, befogged in mind and fatigued in body. I had not the professional enthusiasm which carried my companion on, nor could I look at the matter as a mere abstract intellectual problem. As far as the death of Bartholomew Sholto went, I had heard little good of him, and could feel no intense antipathy to his murderers. The treasure, however, was a different matter. That, or part of it, belonged rightfully to Miss Morstan. While there was a chance of recovering it I was ready to devote my life to the one object. True, if I found it it would probably put her forever beyond my reach. Yet it would be a petty and selfish love which would be influenced by such a thought as that. If Holmes could work to find the criminals, I had a tenfold stronger reason to urge me on to find the treasure.

A bath at Baker Street and a complete change freshened me up wonderfully. When I came down to our room I found the breakfast laid and Homes pouring out the coffee.

"Here it is," said he, laughing, and pointing to an open newspaper. "The energetic Jones and the ubiquitous reporter have fixed it up between them. But you have had enough of the case. Better have your ham and eggs first."

I took the paper from him and read the short notice, which was headed "Mysterious Business at Upper Norwood."

"About twelve o'clock last night," said the Standard, "Mr. Bartholomew Sholto, of Pondicherry Lodge, Upper Norwood, was found dead in his room under circumstances which point to foul play. As far as we can learn, no actual traces of violence were found upon Mr. Sholto's person, but a valuable collection of Indian gems which the deceased gentleman had inherited from his father has been carried off. The discovery was first made by Mr. Sherlock Holmes and Dr. Watson, who had called at the house with Mr. Thaddeus Sholto, brother of the deceased. By a singular piece of good fortune, Mr. Athelney Jones, the well-known member of the detective police force, happened to be at the Norwood Police Station, and was on the ground within half an hour of the first alarm. His trained and experienced faculties were at once directed towards the detection of the criminals, with the gratifying result that the brother, Thaddeus Sholto, has already been arrested, together with the housekeeper, Mrs. Bernstone, an Indian butler named Lal Rao, and a porter, or gatekeeper, named McMurdo. It is quite certain that the thief or thieves were well acquainted with the house, for Mr. Jones's well-known technical knowledge and his powers of minute observation have enabled him to prove conclusively that the miscreants could not have entered by the door or by the window, but must have made their way across the roof of the building, and so through a trap-door into a room which communicated with that in which the body was found. This fact, which has been very clearly made out, proves conclusively that it was no mere haphazard burglary. The prompt and energetic action of the officers of the law shows the great advantage of the presence on such occasions of a single vigorous and masterful mind. We cannot but think that it supplies an argument to those who would wish to see our detectives more decentralized, and so brought into closer and more effective touch with the cases which it is their duty to investigate."

"Isn't it gorgeous!" said Holmes, grinning over his coffee-cup. "What do you think of it?"

"I think that we have had a close shave ourselves of being arrested for the crime."

"So do I. I wouldn't answer for our safety now, if he should happen to have another of his attacks of energy."

At this moment there was a loud ring at the bell, and I could hear Mrs. Hudson, our landlady, raising her voice in a wail of expostulation and dismay.

"By heaven, Holmes," I said, half rising, "I believe that they are really after us."

"No, it's not quite so bad as that. It is the unofficial force,—the Baker Street irregulars."

As he spoke, there came a swift pattering of naked feet upon the stairs, a clatter of high voices, and in rushed a dozen dirty and ragged little street-Arabs. There was some show of discipline among them, despite their tumultuous entry, for they instantly drew up in line and stood facing us with expectant faces. One of their number, taller and older than the others, stood forward with an air of lounging superiority which was very funny in such a disreputable little scarecrow.

"Got your message, sir," said he, "and brought 'em on sharp. Three bob and a tanner for tickets."

"Here you are," said Holmes, producing some silver. "In future they can report to you, Wiggins, and you to me. I cannot have the house invaded in this way. However, it is just as well that you should all hear the instructions. I want to find the whereabouts of a steam launch called the Aurora, owner Mordecai Smith, black with two red streaks, funnel black with a white band. She is down the river somewhere. I want one boy to be at Mordecai Smith's landing-stage opposite Millbank to say if the boat comes back. You must divide it out among yourselves, and do both banks thoroughly. Let me know the moment you have news. Is that all clear?"

"Yes, guv'nor," said Wiggins.

"The old scale of pay, and a guinea to the boy who finds the boat. Here's a day in advance. Now off you go!" He handed them a shilling each, and away they buzzed down the stairs, and I saw them a moment later streaming down the street.

"If the launch is above water they will find her," said Holmes, as he rose from the table and lit his pipe. "They can go everywhere, see everything, overhear every one. I expect to hear before evening that they have spotted her. In the mean while, we can do nothing but await results. We cannot pick up the broken trail until we find either the Aurora or Mr. Mordecai Smith."

"Toby could eat these scraps, I dare say. Are you going to bed, Holmes?"

"No: I am not tired. I have a curious constitution. I never remember feeling tired by work, though idleness exhausts me completely. I am going to smoke and to think over this queer business to which my fair client has introduced us. If ever man had an easy task, this of ours ought to be. Wooden-legged men are not so common, but the other man must, I should think, be absolutely unique."

"That other man again!"

"I have no wish to make a mystery of him,—to you, anyway. But you must have formed your own opinion. Now, do consider the data. Diminutive footmarks, toes never fettered by boots, naked feet, stone-headed wooden mace, great agility, small poisoned darts. What do you make of all this?"

"A savage!" I exclaimed. "Perhaps one of those Indians who were the associates of Jonathan Small."

"Hardly that," said he. "When first I saw signs of strange weapons I was inclined to think so;   but the remarkable character of the footmarks caused me to reconsider my views. Some of the inhabitants of the Indian Peninsula are small men, but none could have left such marks as that. The Hindu proper has long and thin feet. The sandal-wearing Mohammedan has the great toe well separated from the others, because the thong is commonly passed between. These little darts, too, could only be shot in one way. They are from a blow-pipe. Now, then, where are we to find our savage?"

"South American," I hazarded.

He stretched his hand up, and took down a bulky volume from the shelf. "This is the first volume of a gazetteer which is now being published. It may be looked upon as the very latest authority. What have we here? 'Andaman Islands, situated 340 miles to the north of Sumatra, in the Bay of Bengal.' Hum! hum! What's all this? Moist climate, coral reefs, sharks, Port Blair, convict-barracks, Rutland Island, cottonwoods— Ah, here we are. 'The aborigines of the Andaman Islands may perhaps claim the distinction of being the smallest race upon this earth, though some anthropologists prefer the Bushmen of Africa, the Digger Indians of America, and the Terra del Fuegians. The average height is rather below four feet, although many full-grown adults may be found who are very much smaller than this. They are a fierce, morose, and intractable people, though capable of forming most devoted friendships when their confidence has once been gained.' Mark that, Watson. Now, then, listen to this. 'They are naturally hideous, having large, misshapen heads, small, fierce eyes, and distorted features. Their feet and hands, however, are remarkably small. So intractable and fierce are they that all the efforts of the British official have failed to win them over in any degree. They have always been a terror to shipwrecked crews, braining the survivors with their stone-headed clubs, or shooting them with their poisoned arrows. These massacres are invariably concluded by a cannibal feast.' Nice, amiable people, Watson! If this fellow had been left to his own unaided devices this affair might have taken an even more ghastly turn. I fancy that, even as it is, Jonathan Small would give a good deal not to have employed him."

"But how came he to have so singular a companion?"

"Ah, that is more than I can tell. Since, however, we had already determined that Small had come from the Andamans, it is not so very wonderful that this islander should be with him. No doubt we shall know all about it in time. Look here, Watson; you look regularly done. Lie down there on the sofa, and see if I can put you to sleep."

He took up his violin from the corner, and as I stretched myself out he began to play some low, dreamy, melodious air,—his own, no doubt, for he had a remarkable gift for improvisation. I have a vague remembrance of his gaunt limbs, his earnest face, and the rise and fall of his bow. Then I seemed to be floated peacefully away upon a soft sea of sound, until I found myself in dream-land, with the sweet face of Mary Morstan looking down upon me.

9 A Break in the Chain

It was late in the afternoon before I woke, strengthened and refreshed. Sherlock Holmes still sat exactly as I had left him, save that he had laid aside his violin and was deep in a book. He looked across at me, as I stirred, and I noticed that his face was dark and troubled.

"You have slept soundly," he said. "I feared that our talk would wake you."

"I heard nothing," I answered. "Have you had fresh news, then?"

"Unfortunately, no. I confess that I am surprised and disappointed. I expected something definite by this time. Wiggins has just been up to report. He says that no trace can be found of the launch. It is a provoking check, for every hour is of importance."

"Can I do anything? I am perfectly fresh now, and quite ready for another night's outing."

"No, we can do nothing. We can only wait. If we go ourselves, the message might come in our absence, and delay be caused. You can do what you will, but I must remain on guard."

"Then I shall run over to Camberwell and call upon Mrs. Cecil Forrester. She asked me to, yesterday."

"On Mrs. Cecil Forrester?" asked Holmes, with the twinkle of a smile in his eyes.

"Well, of course Miss Morstan too. They were anxious to hear what happened."

"I would not tell them too much," said Holmes. "Women are never to be entirely trusted,—not the best of them."

I did not pause to argue over this atrocious sentiment. "I shall be back in an hour or two," I remarked.

"All right! Good luck! But, I say, if you are crossing the river you may as well return Toby, for I don't think it is at all likely that we shall have any use for him now."

I took our mongrel accordingly, and left him, together with a half-sovereign, at the old naturalist's in Pinchin Lane. At Camberwell I found Miss Morstan a little weary after her night's adventures, but very eager to hear the news. Mrs. Forrester, too, was full of curiosity. I told them all that we had done, suppressing, however, the more dreadful parts of the tragedy. Thus, although I spoke of Mr. Sholto's death, I said nothing of the exact manner and method of it. With all my omissions, however, there was enough to startle and amaze them.

"It is a romance!" cried Mrs. Forrester. "An injured lady, half a million in treasure, a black cannibal, and a wooden-legged ruffian. They take the place of the conventional dragon or wicked earl."

"And two knight-errants to the rescue," added Miss Morstan, with a bright glance at me.

"Why, Mary, your fortune depends upon the issue of this search. I don't think that you are nearly excited enough. Just imagine what it must be to be so rich, and to have the world at your feet!"

It sent a little thrill of joy to my heart to notice that she showed no sign of elation at the prospect. On the contrary, she gave a toss of her proud head, as though the matter were one in which she took small interest.

"It is for Mr. Thaddeus Sholto that I am anxious," she said. "Nothing else is of any consequence;   but I think that he has behaved most kindly and honorably throughout. It is our duty to clear him of this dreadful and unfounded charge."

It was evening before I left Camberwell, and quite dark by the time I reached home. My companion's book and pipe lay by his chair, but he had disappeared. I looked about in the hope of seeing a note, but there was none.

"I suppose that Mr. Sherlock Holmes has gone out," I said to Mrs. Hudson as she came up to lower the blinds.

"No, sir. He has gone to his room, sir. Do you know, sir," sinking her voice into an impressive whisper, "I am afraid for his health?"

"Why so, Mrs. Hudson?"

"Well, he's that strange, sir. After you was gone he walked and he walked, up and down, and up and down, until I was weary of the sound of his footstep. Then I heard him talking to himself and muttering, and every time the bell rang out he came on the stairhead, with 'What is that, Mrs. Hudson?' And now he has slammed off to his room, but I can hear him walking away the same as ever. I hope he's not going to be ill, sir. I ventured to say something to him about cooling medicine, but he turned on me, sir, with such a look that I don't know how ever I got out of the room."

"I don't think that you have any cause to be uneasy, Mrs. Hudson," I answered. "I have seen him like this before. He has some small matter upon his mind which makes him restless." I tried to speak lightly to our worthy landlady, but I was myself somewhat uneasy when through the long night I still from time to time heard the dull sound of his tread, and knew how his keen spirit was chafing against this involuntary inaction.

At breakfast-time he looked worn and haggard, with a little fleck of feverish color upon either cheek.

"You are knocking yourself up, old man," I remarked. "I heard you marching about in the night."

"No, I could not sleep," he answered. "This infernal problem is consuming me. It is too much to be balked by so petty an obstacle, when all else had been overcome. I know the men, the launch, everything;   and yet I can get no news. I have set other agencies at work, and used every means at my disposal. The whole river has been searched on either side, but there is no news, nor has Mrs. Smith heard of her husband. I shall come to the conclusion soon that they have scuttled the craft. But there are objections to that."

"Or that Mrs. Smith has put us on a wrong scent."

"No, I think that may be dismissed. I had inquiries made, and there is a launch of that description."

"Could it have gone up the river?"

"I have considered that possibility too, and there is a search-party who will work up as far as Richmond. If no news comes to-day, I shall start off myself to-morrow, and go for the men rather than the boat. But surely, surely, we shall hear something."

We did not, however. Not a word came to us either from Wiggins or from the other agencies. There were articles in most of the papers upon the Norwood tragedy. They all appeared to be rather hostile to the unfortunate Thaddeus Sholto. No fresh details were to be found, however, in any of them, save that an inquest was to be held upon the following day. I walked over to Camberwell in the evening to report our ill success to the ladies, and on my return I found Holmes dejected and somewhat morose. He would hardly reply to my questions, and busied himself all evening in an abstruse chemical analysis which involved much heating of retorts and distilling of vapors, ending at last in a smell which fairly drove me out of the apartment. Up to the small hours of the morning I could hear the clinking of his test-tubes which told me that he was still engaged in his malodorous experiment.

In the early dawn I woke with a start, and was surprised to find him standing by my bedside, clad in a rude sailor dress with a pea-jacket, and a coarse red scarf round his neck.

"I am off down the river, Watson," said he. "I have been turning it over in my mind, and I can see only one way out of it. It is worth trying, at all events."

"Surely I can come with you, then?" said I.

"No; you can be much more useful if you will remain here as my representative. I am loath to go, for it is quite on the cards that some message may come during the day, though Wiggins was despondent about it last night. I want you to open all notes and telegrams, and to act on your own judgment if any news should come. Can I rely upon you?"

"Most certainly."

"I am afraid that you will not be able to wire to me, for I can hardly tell yet where I may find myself. If I am in luck, however, I may not be gone so very long. I shall have news of some sort or other before I get back."

I had heard nothing of him by breakfast-time. On opening the Standard, however, I found that there was a fresh allusion to the business. "With reference to the Upper Norwood tragedy," it remarked, "we have reason to believe that the matter promises to be even more complex and mysterious than was originally supposed. Fresh evidence has shown that it is quite impossible that Mr. Thaddeus Sholto could have been in any way concerned in the matter. He and the housekeeper, Mrs. Bernstone, were both released yesterday evening. It is believed, however, that the police have a clue as to the real culprits, and that it is being prosecuted by Mr. Athelney Jones, of Scotland Yard, with all his well-known energy and sagacity. Further arrests may be expected at any moment."

"That is satisfactory so far as it goes," thought I. "Friend Sholto is safe, at any rate. I wonder what the fresh clue may be;   though it seems to be a stereotyped form whenever the police have made a blunder."

I tossed the paper down upon the table, but at that moment my eye caught an advertisement in the agony column. It ran in this way:

"Lost.—Whereas Mordecai Smith, boatman, and his son, Jim, left Smith's Wharf at or about three o'clock last Tuesday morning in the steam launch Aurora, black with two red stripes, funnel black with a white band, the sum of five pounds will be paid to any one who can give information to Mrs. Smith, at Smith's Wharf, or at 221B Baker Street, as to the whereabouts of the said Mordecai Smith and the launch Aurora."

This was clearly Holmes's doing. The Baker Street address was enough to prove that. It struck me as rather ingenious, because it might be read by the fugitives without their seeing in it more than the natural anxiety of a wife for her missing husband.

It was a long day. Every time that a knock came to the door, or a sharp step passed in the street, I imagined that it was either Holmes returning or an answer to his advertisement. I tried to read, but my thoughts would wander off to our strange quest and to the ill-assorted and villainous pair whom we were pursuing. Could there be, I wondered, some radical flaw in my companion's reasoning. Might he be suffering from some huge self-deception? Was it not possible that his nimble and speculative mind had built up this wild theory upon faulty premises? I had never known him to be wrong; and yet the keenest reasoner may occasionally be deceived. He was likely, I thought, to fall into error through the over-refinement of his logic,—his preference for a subtle and bizarre explanation when a plainer and more commonplace one lay ready to his hand. Yet, on the other hand, I had myself seen the evidence, and I had heard the reasons for his deductions. When I looked back on the long chain of curious circumstances, many of them trivial in themselves, but all tending in the same direction, I could not disguise from myself that even if Holmes's explanation were incorrect the true theory must be equally outre and startling.

At three o'clock in the afternoon there was a loud peal at the bell, an authoritative voice in the hall, and, to my surprise, no less a person than Mr. Athelney Jones was shown up to me. Very different was he, however, from the brusque and masterful professor of common sense who had taken over the case so confidently at Upper Norwood. His expression was downcast, and his bearing meek and even apologetic.

"Good-day, sir; good-day," said he. "Mr. Sherlock Holmes is out, I understand."

"Yes, and I cannot be sure when he will be back. But perhaps you would care to wait. Take that chair and try one of these cigars."

"Thank you;   I don't mind if I do," said he, mopping his face with a red bandanna handkerchief.

"And a whiskey-and-soda?"

"Well, half a glass. It is very hot for the time of year; and I have had a good deal to worry and try me. You know my theory about this Norwood case?"

"I remember that you expressed one."

"Well, I have been obliged to reconsider it. I had my net drawn tightly round Mr. Sholto, sir, when pop he went through a hole in the middle of it. He was able to prove an alibi which could not be shaken. From the time that he left his brother's room he was never out of sight of some one or other. So it could not be he who climbed over roofs and through trap-doors. It's a very dark case, and my professional credit is at stake. I should be very glad of a little assistance."

"We all need help sometimes," said I.

"Your friend Mr. Sherlock Holmes is a wonderful man, sir," said he, in a husky and confidential voice. "He's a man who is not to be beat. I have known that young man go into a good many cases, but I never saw the case yet that he could not throw a light upon. He is irregular in his methods, and a little quick perhaps in jumping at theories, but, on the whole, I think he would have made a most promising officer, and I don't care who knows it. I have had a wire from him this morning, by which I understand that he has got some clue to this Sholto business. Here is the message."

He took the telegram out of his pocket, and handed it to me. It was dated from Poplar at twelve o'clock. "Go to Baker Street at once," it said. "If I have not returned, wait for me. I am close on the track of the Sholto gang. You can come with us to-night if you want to be in at the finish."

195

"This sounds well. He has evidently picked up the scent again," said I.

"Ah, then he has been at fault too," exclaimed Jones, with evident satisfaction. "Even the best of us are thrown off sometimes. Of course this may prove to be a false alarm; but it is my duty as an officer of the law to allow no chance to slip. But there is some one at the door. Perhaps this is he."

A heavy step was heard ascending the stair, with a great wheezing and rattling as from a man who was sorely put to it for breath. Once or twice he stopped, as though the climb were too much for him, but at last he made his way to our door and entered. His appearance corresponded to the sounds which we had heard. He was an aged man, clad in seafaring garb, with an old pea-jacket buttoned up to his throat. His back was bowed, his knees were shaky, and his breathing was painfully asthmatic. As he leaned upon a thick oaken cudgel his shoulders heaved in the effort to draw the air into his lungs. He had a colored scarf round his chin, and I could see little of his face save a pair of keen dark eyes, overhung by bushy white brows, and long gray side-whiskers. Altogether he gave me the impression of a respectable master mariner who had fallen into years and poverty.

"What is it, my man?" I asked.

He looked about him in the slow methodical fashion of old age.

"Is Mr. Sherlock Holmes here?" said he.

"No; but I am acting for him. You can tell me any message you have for him."

"It was to him himself I was to tell it," said he.

"But I tell you that I am acting for him. Was it about Mordecai Smith's boat?"

"Yes. I knows well where it is. An' I knows where the men he is after are. An' I knows where the treasure is. I knows all about it."

"Then tell me, and I shall let him know."

"It was to him I was to tell it," he repeated, with the petulant obstinacy of a very old man.

"Well, you must wait for him."

"No, no; I ain't goin' to lose a whole day to please no one. If Mr. Holmes ain't here, then Mr. Holmes must find it all out for himself. I don't care about the look of either of you, and I won't tell a word."

He shuffled towards the door, but Athelney Jones got in front of him.

"Wait a bit, my friend," said he. "You have important information, and you must not walk off. We shall keep you, whether you like or not, until our friend returns."

The old man made a little run towards the door, but, as Athelney Jones put his broad back up against it, he recognized the uselessness of resistance.

"Pretty sort o' treatment this!" he cried, stamping his stick. "I come here to see a gentleman, and you two, who I never saw in my life, seize me and treat me in this fashion!"

"You will be none the worse," I said. "We shall recompense you for the loss of your time. Sit over here on the sofa, and you will not have long to wait."

He came across sullenly enough, and seated himself with his face resting on his hands. Jones and I resumed our cigars and our talk. Suddenly, however, Holmes's voice broke in upon us.

"I think that you might offer me a cigar too," he said.

We both started in our chairs. There was Holmes sitting close to us with an air of quiet amusement.

"Holmes!" I exclaimed. "You here! But where is the old man?"

"Here is the old man," said he, holding out a heap of white hair. "Here he is,—wig, whiskers, eyebrows, and all. I thought my disguise was pretty good, but I hardly expected that it would stand that test."

"Ah, You rogue!" cried Jones, highly delighted. "You would have made an actor, and a rare one. You had the proper workhouse cough, and those weak legs of yours are worth ten pound a week. I thought I knew the glint of your eye, though. You didn't get away from us so easily, You see."

"I have been working in that get-up all day," said he, lighting his cigar. "You see, a good many of the criminal classes begin to know me,—especially since our friend here took to publishing some of my cases: so I can only go on the war-path under some simple disguise like this. You got my wire?"

"Yes;   that was what brought me here."

"How has your case prospered?"

"It has all come to nothing. I have had to release two of my prisoners, and there is no evidence against the other two."

"Never mind. We shall give you two others in the place of them. But you must put yourself under my orders. You are welcome to all the official credit, but you must act on the line that I point out. Is that agreed?"

"Entirely, if you will help me to the men."

"Well, then, in the first place I shall want a fast police-boat—a steam launch—to be at the Westminster Stairs at seven o'clock."

"That is easily managed. There is always one about there; but I can step across the road and telephone to make sure."

"Then I shall want two stanch men, in case of resistance."

"There will be two or three in the boat. What else?"

"When we secure the men we shall get the treasure. I think that it would be a pleasure to my friend here to take the box round to the young lady to whom half of it rightfully belongs. Let her be the first to open it.—Eh, Watson?"

"It would be a great pleasure to me."

"Rather an irregular proceeding," said Jones, shaking his head. "However, the whole thing is irregular, and I suppose we must wink at it. The treasure must afterwards be handed over to the authorities until after the official investigation."

"Certainly. That is easily managed. One other point. I should much like to have a few details about this matter from the lips of Jonathan Small himself. You know I like to work the detail of my cases out. There is no objection to my having an unofficial interview with him, either here in my rooms or elsewhere, as long as he is efficiently guarded?"

"Well, you are master of the situation. I have had no proof yet of the existence of this Jonathan Small. However, if you can catch him I don't see how I can refuse you an interview with him."

"That is understood, then?"

"Perfectly. Is there anything else?"

"Only that I insist upon your dining with us. It will be ready in half an hour. I have oysters and a brace of grouse, with something a little choice in white wines.—Watson, you have never yet recognized my merits as a housekeeper."

10 The End of the Islander

Our meal was a merry one. Holmes could talk exceedingly well when he chose, and that night he did choose. He appeared to be in a state of nervous exaltation. I have never known him so brilliant. He spoke on a quick succession of subjects,—on miracle-plays, on medieval pottery, on Stradivarius violins, on the Buddhism of Ceylon, and on the war-ships of the future,—handling each as though he had made a special study of it. His bright humor marked the reaction from his black depression of the preceding days. Athelney Jones proved to be a sociable soul in his hours of relaxation, and faced his dinner with the air of a bon vivant. For myself, I felt elated at the thought that we were nearing the end of our task, and I caught something of Holmes's gaiety. None of us alluded during dinner to the cause which had brought us together.

When the cloth was cleared, Holmes glanced at his watch, and filled up three glasses with port. "One bumper," said he, "to the success of our little expedition. And now it is high time we were off. Have you a pistol, Watson?"

"I have my old service-revolver in my desk."

"You had best take it, then. It is well to be prepared. I see that the cab is at the door. I ordered it for half-past six."

It was a little past seven before we reached the Westminster wharf, and found our launch awaiting us. Holmes eyed it critically.

"Is there anything to mark it as a police-boat?"

"Yes,—that green lamp at the side."

"Then take it off."

The small change was made, we stepped on board, and the ropes were cast off. Jones, Holmes, and I sat in the stern. There was one man at the rudder, one to tend the engines, and two burly police-inspectors forward.

"Where to?" asked Jones.

"To the Tower. Tell them to stop opposite Jacobson's Yard."

Our craft was evidently a very fast one. We shot past the long lines of loaded barges as though they were stationary. Holmes smiled with satisfaction as we overhauled a river steamer and left her behind us.

"We ought to be able to catch anything on the river," he said.

"Well, hardly that. But there are not many launches to beat us."

"We shall have to catch the Aurora, and she has a name for being a clipper. I will tell you how the land lies, Watson. You recollect how annoyed I was at being balked by so small a thing?"

"Yes."

"Well, I gave my mind a thorough rest by plunging into a chemical analysis. One of our greatest statesmen has said that a change of work is the best rest. So it is. When I had succeeded in dissolving the hydrocarbon which I was at work at, I came back to our problem of the Sholtos, and thought the whole matter out again. My boys had been up the river and down the river without result. The launch was not at any landing-stage or wharf, nor had it returned. Yet it could hardly have been scuttled to hide their traces,—though that always remained as a possible hypothesis if all else failed. I knew this man Small had a certain degree of low cunning, but I did not think him capable of anything in the nature of delicate finesse. That is usually a product of higher education. I then reflected that since he had certainly been in London some time—as we had evidence that he maintained a continual watch over Pondicherry Lodge—he could hardly leave at a moment's notice, but would need some little time, if it were only a day, to arrange his affairs. That was the balance of probability, at any rate."

"It seems to me to be a little weak," said I. "It is more probable that he had arranged his affairs before ever he set out upon his expedition."

"No, I hardly think so. This lair of his would be too valuable a retreat in case of need for him to give it up until he was sure that he could do without it. But a second consideration struck me. Jonathan Small must have felt that the peculiar appearance of his companion, however much he may have top-coated him, would give rise to gossip, and possibly be associated with this Norwood tragedy. He was quite sharp enough to see that. They had started from their head-quarters under cover of darkness, and he would wish to get back before it was broad light. Now, it was past three o'clock, according to Mrs. Smith, when they got the boat. It would be quite bright, and people would be about in an hour or so. Therefore, I argued, they did not go very far. They paid Smith well to hold his tongue, reserved his launch for the final escape, and hurried to their lodgings with the treasure-box. In a couple of nights, when they had time to see what view the papers took, and whether there was any suspicion, they would make their way under cover of darkness to some ship at Gravesend or in the Downs, where no doubt they had already arranged for passages to America or the Colonies."

"But the launch? They could not have taken that to their lodgings."

"Quite so. I argued that the launch must be no great way off, in spite of its invisibility. I then put myself in the place of Small, and looked at it as a man of his capacity would. He would probably consider that to send back the launch or to keep it at a wharf would make pursuit easy if the police did happen to get on his track. How, then, could he conceal the launch and yet have her at hand when wanted? I wondered what I should do myself if I were in his shoes. I could only think of one way of doing it. I might land the launch over to some boat-builder or repairer, with directions to make a trifling change in her. She would then be removed to his shed or yard, and so be effectually concealed, while at the same time I could have her at a few hours' notice."

"That seems simple enough."

"It is just these very simple things which are extremely liable to be overlooked. However, I determined to act on the idea. I started at once in this harmless seaman's rig and inquired at all the yards down the river. I drew blank at fifteen, but at the sixteenth—Jacobson's—I learned that the Aurora had been handed over to them two days ago by a wooden-legged man, with some trivial directions as to her rudder. 'There ain't naught amiss with her rudder,' said the foreman. 'There she lies, with the red streaks.' At that moment who should come down but Mordecai Smith, the missing owner? He was rather the worse for liquor. I should not, of course, have known him, but he bellowed out his name and the name of his launch. 'I want her to-night at eight o'clock,' said he,—'eight o'clock sharp, mind, for I have two gentlemen who won't be kept waiting.' They had evidently paid him well, for he was very flush of money, chucking shillings about to the men. I followed him some distance, but he subsided into an ale-house: so I went back to the yard, and, happening to pick up one of my boys on the way, I stationed him as a sentry over the launch. He is to stand at water's edge and wave his handkerchief to us when they start. We shall be lying off in the stream, and it will be a strange thing if we do not take men, treasure, and all."

"You have planned it all very neatly, whether they are the right men or not," said Jones; "but if the affair were in my hands I should have had a body of police in Jacobson's Yard, and arrested them when they came down."

"Which would have been never. This man Small is a pretty shrewd fellow. He would send a scout on ahead, and if anything made him suspicious lie snug for another week."

"But you might have stuck to Mordecai Smith, and so been led to their hiding-place," said I.

"In that case I should have wasted my day. I think that it is a hundred to one against Smith knowing where they live. As long as he has liquor and good pay, why should he ask questions? They send him messages what to do. No, I thought over every possible course, and this is the best."

While this conversation had been proceeding, we had been shooting the long series of bridges which span the Thames. As we passed the City the last rays of the sun were gilding the cross upon the summit of St. Paul's. It was twilight before we reached the Tower.

"That is Jacobson's Yard," said Holmes, pointing to a bristle of masts and rigging on the Surrey side. "Cruise gently up and down here under cover of this string of lighters." He took a pair of night-glasses from his pocket and gazed some time at the shore. "I see my sentry at his post," he remarked, "but no sign of a handkerchief."

"Suppose we go down-stream a short way and lie in wait for them," said Jones, eagerly. We were all eager by this time, even the policemen and stokers, who had a very vague idea of what was going forward.

"We have no right to take anything for granted," Holmes answered. "It is certainly ten to one that they go down-stream, but we cannot be certain. From this point we can see the entrance of the yard, and they can hardly see us. It will be a clear night and plenty of light. We must stay where we are. See how the folk swarm over yonder in the gaslight."

"They are coming from work in the yard."

"Dirty-looking rascals, but I suppose every one has some little immortal spark concealed about him. You would not think it, to look at them. There is no a priori probability about it. A strange enigma is man!"

"Some one calls him a soul concealed in an animal," I suggested.

"Winwood Reade is good upon the subject," said Holmes. "He remarks that, while the individual man is an insoluble puzzle, in the aggregate he becomes a mathematical certainty. You can, for example, never foretell what any one man will do, but you can say with precision what an average number will be up to. Individuals vary, but percentages remain constant. So says the statistician. But do I see a handkerchief? Surely there is a white flutter over yonder."

"Yes, it is your boy," I cried. "I can see him plainly."

"And there is the Aurora," exclaimed Holmes, "and going like the devil! Full speed ahead, engineer. Make after that launch with the yellow light. By heaven, I shall never forgive myself if she proves to have the heels of us!"

She had slipped unseen through the yard-entrance and passed behind two or three small craft, so that she had fairly got her speed up before we saw her. Now she was flying down the stream, near in to the shore, going at a tremendous rate. Jones looked gravely at her and shook his head.

"She is very fast," he said. "I doubt if we shall catch her."

"We MUST catch her!" cried Holmes, between his teeth. "Heap it on, stokers! Make her do all she can! If we burn the boat we must have them!"

We were fairly after her now. The furnaces roared, and the powerful engines whizzed and clanked, like a great metallic heart. Her sharp, steep prow cut through the river-water and sent two rolling waves to right and to left of us. With every throb of the engines we sprang and quivered like a living thing. One great yellow lantern in our bows threw a long, flickering funnel of light in front of us. Right ahead a dark blur upon the water showed where the Aurora lay, and the swirl of white foam behind her spoke of the pace at which she was going. We flashed past barges, steamers, merchant-vessels, in and out, behind this one and round the other. Voices hailed us out of the darkness, but still the Aurora thundered on, and still we followed close upon her track.

"Pile it on, men, pile it on!" cried Holmes, looking down into the engine-room, while the fierce glow from below beat upon his eager, aquiline face. "Get every pound of steam you can."

"I think we gain a little," said Jones, with his eyes on the Aurora.

"I am sure of it," said I. "We shall be up with her in a very few minutes."

At that moment, however, as our evil fate would have it, a tug with three barges in tow blundered in between us. It was only by putting our helm hard down that we avoided a collision, and before we could round them and recover our way the Aurora had gained a good two hundred yards. She was still, however, well in view, and the murky uncertain twilight was setting into a clear starlit night. Our boilers were strained to their utmost, and the frail shell vibrated and creaked with the fierce energy which was driving us along. We had shot through the Pool, past the West India Docks, down the long Deptford Reach, and up again after rounding the Isle of Dogs. The dull blur in front of us resolved itself now clearly enough into the dainty Aurora. Jones turned our search-light upon her, so that we could plainly see the figures upon her deck. One man sat by the stern, with something black between his knees over which he stooped. Beside him lay a dark mass which looked like a Newfoundland dog. The boy held the tiller, while against the red glare of the furnace I could see old Smith, stripped to the waist, and shoveling coals for dear life. They may have had some doubt at first as to whether we were really pursuing them, but now as we followed every winding and turning which they took there could no longer be any question about it. At Greenwich we were about three hundred paces behind them. At Blackwall we could not have been more than two hundred and fifty. I have coursed many creatures in many countries during my checkered career, but never did sport give me such a wild thrill as this mad, flying man-hunt down the Thames. Steadily we drew in upon them, yard by yard. In the silence of the night we could hear the panting and clanking of their machinery. The man in the stern still crouched upon the deck, and his arms were moving as though he were busy, while every now and then he would look up and measure with a glance the distance which still separated us. Nearer we came and nearer. Jones yelled to them to stop. We were not more than four boat's lengths behind them, both boats flying at a tremendous pace. It was a clear reach of the river, with Barking Level upon one side and the melancholy Plumstead Marshes upon the other. At our hail the man in the stern sprang up from the deck and shook his two clinched fists at us, cursing the while in a high, cracked voice. He was a good-sized, powerful man, and as he stood poising himself with legs astride I could see that from the thigh downwards there was but a wooden stump upon the right side. At the sound of his strident, angry cries there was movement in the huddled bundle upon the deck. It straightened itself into a little black man—the smallest I have ever seen—with a great, misshapen head and a shock of tangled, disheveled hair. Holmes had already drawn his revolver, and I whipped out mine at the sight of this savage, distorted creature. He was wrapped in some sort of dark ulster or blanket, which left only his face exposed; but that face was enough to give a man a sleepless night. Never have I seen features so deeply marked with all bestiality and cruelty. His small eyes glowed and burned with a somber light, and his thick lips were writhed back from his teeth, which grinned and chattered at us with a half animal fury.

"Fire if he raises his hand," said Holmes, quietly. We were within a boat's-length by this time, and almost within touch of our quarry. I can see the two of them now as they stood, the white man with his legs far apart, shrieking out curses, and the unhallowed dwarf with his hideous face, and his strong yellow teeth gnashing at us in the light of our lantern.

It was well that we had so clear a view of him. Even as

we looked he plucked out from under his covering a short, round piece of wood, like a school-ruler, and clapped it to his lips. Our pistols rang out together. He whirled round, threw up his arms, and with a kind of choking cough fell sideways into the stream. I caught one glimpse of his venomous, menacing eyes amid the white swirl of the waters. At the same moment the wooden-legged man threw himself upon the rudder and put it hard down, so that his boat made straight in for the southern bank, while we shot past her stern, only clearing her by a few feet. We were round after her in an instant, but she was already nearly at the bank. It was a wild and desolate place, where the moon glimmered upon a wide expanse of marsh-land, with pools of stagnant water and beds of decaying vegetation. The launch with a dull thud ran up upon the mud-bank, with her bow in the air and her stern flush with the water. The fugitive sprang out, but his stump instantly sank its whole length into the sodden soil. In vain he struggled and writhed. Not one step could he possibly take either forwards or backwards. He yelled in impotent rage, and kicked frantically into the mud with his other foot, but his struggles only bored his wooden pin the deeper into the sticky bank. When we brought our launch alongside he was so firmly anchored that it was only by throwing the end of a rope over his shoulders that we were able to haul him out, and to drag him, like some evil fish, over our side. The two Smiths, father and son, sat sullenly in their launch, but came aboard meekly enough when commanded. The Aurora herself we hauled off and made fast to our stern. A solid iron chest of Indian workmanship stood upon the deck. This, there could be no question, was the same that had contained the ill-omened treasure of the Sholtos. There was no key, but it was of considerable weight, so we transferred it carefully to our own little cabin. As we steamed slowly up-stream again, we flashed our search-light in every direction, but there was no sign of the Islander. Somewhere in the dark ooze at the bottom of the Thames lie the bones of that strange visitor to our shores.

"See here," said Holmes, pointing to the wooden hatchway. "We were hardly quick enough with our pistols." There, sure enough, just behind where we had been standing, stuck one of those murderous darts which we knew so well. It must have whizzed between us at the instant that we fired. Holmes smiled at it and shrugged his shoulders in his easy fashion, but I confess that it turned me sick to think of the horrible death which had passed so close to us that night.

11 The Great Agra Treasure

Our captive sat in the cabin opposite to the iron box which he had done so much and waited so long to gain. He was a sunburned, reckless-eyed fellow, with a net-work of lines and wrinkles all over his mahogany features, which told of a hard, open-air life. There was a singular prominence about his bearded chin which marked a man who was not to be easily turned from his purpose. His age may have been fifty or thereabouts, for his black, curly hair was thickly shot with gray. His face in repose was not an unpleasing one, though his heavy brows and aggressive chin gave him, as I had lately seen, a terrible expression when moved to anger. He sat now with his handcuffed hands upon his lap, and his head sunk upon his breast, while he looked with his keen, twinkling eyes at the box which had been the cause of his ill-doings. It seemed to me that there was more sorrow than anger in his rigid and contained countenance. Once he looked up at me with a gleam of something like humor in his eyes.

"Well, Jonathan Small," said Holmes, lighting a cigar, "I am sorry that it has come to this."

"And so am I, sir," he answered, frankly. "I don't believe that I can swing over the job. I give you my word on the book that I never raised hand against Mr. Sholto. It was that little hell-hound Tonga who shot one of his cursed darts into him. I had no part in it, sir. I was as grieved as if it had been my blood-relation. I welted the little devil with the slack end of the rope for it, but it was done, and I could not undo it again."

"Have a cigar," said Holmes;   "and you had best take a pull out of my flask, for you are very wet. How could you expect so small and weak a man as this black fellow to overpower Mr. Sholto and hold him while you were climbing the rope?"

"You seem to know as much about it as if you were there, sir. The truth is that I hoped to find the room clear. I knew the habits of the house pretty well, and it was the time when Mr. Sholto usually went down to his supper. I shall make no secret of the business. The best defense that I can make is just the simple truth. Now, if it had been the old major I would have swung for him with a light heart. I would have thought no more of knifing him than of smoking this cigar. But it's cursed hard that I should be lagged over this young Sholto, with whom I had no quarrel whatever."

"You are under the charge of Mr. Athelney Jones, of Scotland Yard. He is going to bring you up to my rooms, and I shall ask you for a true account of the matter. You must make a clean breast of it, for if you do I hope that I may be of use to you. I think I can prove that the poison acts so quickly that the man was dead before ever you reached the room."

"That he was, sir. I never got such a turn in my life as when I saw him grinning at me with his head on his shoulder as I climbed through the window. It fairly shook me, sir. I'd have half killed Tonga for it if he had not scrambled off. That was how he came to leave his club, and some of his darts too, as he tells me, which I dare say helped to put you on our track;   though how you kept on it is more than I can tell. I don't feel no malice against you for it. But it does seem a queer thing," he added, with a bitter smile, "that I who have a fair claim to nigh upon half a million of money should spend the first half of my life building a breakwater in the

Andamans, and am like to spend the other half digging drains at Dartmoor. It was an evil day for me when first I clapped eyes upon the merchant Achmet and had to do with the Agra treasure, which never brought anything but a curse yet upon the man who owned it. To him it brought murder, to Major Sholto it brought fear and guilt, to me it has meant slavery for life."

At this moment Athelney Jones thrust his broad face and heavy shoulders into the tiny cabin. "Quite a family party," he remarked. "I think I shall have a pull at that flask, Holmes. Well, I think we may all congratulate each other. Pity we didn't take the other alive; but there was no choice. I say, Holmes, you must confess that you cut it rather fine. It was all we could do to overhaul her."

"All is well that ends well," said Holmes. "But I certainly did not know that the Aurora was such a clipper."

"Smith says she is one of the fastest launches on the river, and that if he had had another man to help him with the engines we should never have caught her. He swears he knew nothing of this Norwood business."

"Neither he did," cried our prisoner,—"not a word. I chose his launch because I heard that she was a flier. We told him nothing, but we paid him well, and he was to get something handsome if we reached our vessel, the Esmeralda, at Gravesend, outward bound for the Brazils."

"Well, if he has done no wrong we shall see that no wrong comes to him. If we are pretty quick in catching our men, we are not so quick in condemning them." It was amusing to notice how the consequential Jones was already beginning to give himself airs on the strength of the capture. From the slight smile which played over Sherlock Holmes's face, I could see that the speech had not been lost upon him.

"We will be at Vauxhall Bridge presently," said Jones, "and shall land you, Dr. Watson, with the treasure-box. I need hardly tell you that I am taking a very grave responsibility upon myself in doing this. It is most irregular; but of course an agreement is an agreement. I must, however, as a matter of duty, send an inspector with you, since you have so valuable a charge. You will drive, no doubt?"

"Yes, I shall drive."

"It is a pity there is no key, that we may make an inventory first. You will have to break it open. Where is the key, my man?"

"At the bottom of the river," said Small, shortly.

"Hum! There was no use your giving this unnecessary trouble. We have had work enough already through you. However, doctor, I need not warn you to be careful. Bring the box back with you to the Baker Street rooms. You will find us there, on our way to the station."

They landed me at Vauxhall, with my heavy iron box, and with a bluff, genial inspector as my companion. A quarter of an hour's drive brought us to Mrs. Cecil Forrester's. The servant seemed surprised at so late a visitor. Mrs. Cecil Forrester was out for the evening, she explained, and likely to be very late. Miss Morstan, however, was in the drawing-room: so to the drawing-room I went, box in hand, leaving the obliging inspector in the cab.

She was seated by the open window, dressed in some sort of white diaphanous material, with a little touch of scarlet at the neck and waist. The soft light of a shaded lamp fell upon her as she leaned back in the basket chair, playing over her sweet, grave face, and tinting with a dull, metallic sparkle the rich coils of her luxuriant hair. One white arm and hand drooped over the side of the chair, and her whole pose and figure spoke of an absorbing melancholy. At the sound of my foot-fall she sprang to her feet, however, and a bright flush of surprise and of pleasure colored her pale cheeks.

"I heard a cab drive up," she said. "I thought that Mrs. Forrester had come back very early, but I never dreamed that it might be you. What news have you brought me?"

"I have brought something better than news," said I, putting down the box upon the table and speaking jovially and boisterously, though my heart was heavy within me. "I have brought you something which is worth all the news in the world. I have brought you a fortune."

She glanced at the iron box. "Is that the treasure, then?" she asked, coolly enough.

"Yes, this is the great Agra treasure. Half of it is yours and half is Thaddeus Sholto's. You will have a couple of hundred thousand each. Think of that! An annuity of ten thousand pounds. There will be few richer young ladies in England. Is it not glorious?"

I think that I must have been rather overacting my delight, and that she detected a hollow ring in my congratulations, for I saw her eyebrows rise a little, and she glanced at me curiously.

"If I have it," said she, "I owe it to you."

"No, no," I answered, "not to me, but to my friend Sherlock Holmes. With all the will in the world, I could never have followed up a clue which has taxed even his analytical genius. As it was, we very nearly lost it at the last moment."

"Pray sit down and tell me all about it, Dr. Watson," said she.

I narrated briefly what had occurred since I had seen her last,—Holmes's new method of search, the discovery of the Aurora, the appearance of Athelney Jones, our expedition in the evening, and the wild chase down the Thames. She listened with parted lips and shining eyes to my recital of our adventures. When I spoke of the dart which had so narrowly missed us, she turned so white that I feared that she was about to faint.

"It is nothing," she said, as I hastened to pour her out some water. "I am all right again. It was a shock to me to hear that I had placed my friends in such horrible peril."

"That is all over," I answered. "It was nothing. I will tell you no more gloomy details. Let us turn to something brighter. There is the treasure. What could be brighter than that? I got leave to bring it with me, thinking that it would interest you to be the first to see it."

"It would be of the greatest interest to me," she said. There was no eagerness in her voice, however. It had struck her, doubtless, that it might seem ungracious upon her part to be indifferent to a prize which had cost so much to win.

"What a pretty box!" she said, stooping over it. "This is Indian work, I suppose?"

"Yes;   it is Benares metal-work."

"And so heavy!" she exclaimed, trying to raise it. "The box alone must be of some value. Where is the key?"

"Small threw it into the Thames," I answered. "I must borrow Mrs. Forrester's poker." There was in the front a thick and broad hasp, wrought in the image of a sitting Buddha. Under this I thrust the end of the poker and twisted it outward as a lever. The hasp sprang open with a loud snap.

With trembling fingers I flung back the lid. We both stood gazing in astonishment. The box was empty!

No wonder that it was heavy. The iron-work was two-thirds of an inch thick all round. It was massive, well made, and solid, like a chest constructed to carry things of great price, but not one shred or crumb of metal or jewelry lay within it. It was absolutely and completely empty.

"The treasure is lost," said Miss Morstan, calmly.

As I listened to the words and realized what they meant, a great shadow seemed to pass from my soul. I did not know how this Agra treasure had weighed me down, until now that it was finally removed. It was selfish, no doubt, disloyal, wrong, but I could realize nothing save that the golden barrier was gone from between us. "Thank God!" I ejaculated from my very heart.

She looked at me with a quick, questioning smile. "Why do you say that?" she asked.

"Because you are within my reach again," I said, taking her hand. She did not withdraw it. "Because I love you, Mary, as truly as ever a man loved a woman. Because this treasure, these riches, sealed my lips. Now that they are gone I can tell you how I love you. That is why I said, 'Thank God.'"

"Then I say, 'Thank God,' too," she whispered, as I drew her to my side. Whoever had lost a treasure, I knew that night that I had gained one.

12 The Strange Story of Jonathan Small

A very patient man was that inspector in the cab, for it was a weary time before I rejoined him. His face clouded over when I showed him the empty box.

"There goes the reward!" said he, gloomily. "Where there is no money there is no pay. This night's work would have been worth a tenner each to Sam Brown and me if the treasure had been there."

"Mr. Thaddeus Sholto is a rich man," I said. "He will see that you are rewarded, treasure or no."

The inspector shook his head despondently, however. "It's a bad job," he repeated;   "and so Mr. Athelney Jones will think."

His forecast proved to be correct, for the detective looked blank enough when I got to Baker Street and showed him the empty box. They had only just arrived, Holmes, the prisoner, and he, for they had changed their plans so far as to report themselves at a station upon the way. My companion lounged in his arm-chair with his usual listless expression, while Small sat stolidly opposite to him with his wooden leg cocked over his sound one. As I exhibited the empty box he leaned back in his chair and laughed aloud.

"This is your doing, Small," said Athelney Jones, angrily.

"Yes, I have put it away where you shall never lay hand upon it," he cried, exultantly. "It is my treasure;   and if I can't have the loot I'll take darned good care that no one else does. I tell you that no living man has any right to it, unless it is three men who are in the Andaman convict-barracks and myself. I know now that I cannot have the use of it, and I know that they cannot. I have acted all through for them as much as for myself. It's been the sign of four with us always. Well I know that they would have had me do just what I have done, and throw the treasure into the Thames rather than let it go to kith or kin of Sholto or of Morstan. It was not to make them rich that we did for Achmet. You'll find the treasure where the key is, and where little Tonga is. When I saw that your launch must catch us, I put the loot away in a safe place. There are no rupees for you this journey."

"You are deceiving us, Small," said Athelney Jones, sternly. "If you had wished to throw the treasure into the Thames it would have been easier for you to have thrown box and all."

"Easier for me to throw, and easier for you to recover," he answered, with a shrewd, sidelong look. "The man that was clever enough to hunt me down is clever enough to pick an iron box from the bottom of a river. Now that they are scattered over five miles or so, it may be a harder job. It went to my heart to do it, though. I was half mad when you came up with us. However, there's no good grieving over it. I've had ups in my life, and I've had downs, but I've learned not to cry over spilled milk."

"This is a very serious matter, Small," said the detective. "If you had helped justice, instead of thwarting it in this way, you would have had a better chance at your trial."

"Justice!" snarled the ex-convict. "A pretty justice! Whose loot is this, if it is not ours? Where is the justice that I should give it up to those who have never earned it? Look how I have earned it! Twenty long years in that fever-ridden swamp, all day at work under the mangrove-tree, all night chained up in the filthy convict-huts, bitten by mosquitoes, racked with ague, bullied by every cursed black-faced policeman who loved to take it out of a white man. That was how I earned the Agra treasure; and you talk to me of justice because I cannot bear to feel that I have paid this price only that another may enjoy it! I would rather swing a score of times, or have one of Tonga's darts in my hide, than live in a convict's cell and feel that another man is at his ease in a palace with the money that should be mine." Small had dropped his mask of stoicism, and all this came out in a wild whirl of words, while his eyes blazed, and the handcuffs clanked together with the impassioned movement of his hands. I could understand, as I saw the fury and the passion of the man, that it was no groundless or unnatural terror which had possessed Major Sholto when he first learned that the injured convict was upon his track.

"You forget that we know nothing of all this," said Holmes quietly. "We have not heard your story, and we cannot tell how far justice may originally have been on your side."

"Well, sir, you have been very fair-spoken to me, though I can see that I have you to thank that I have these bracelets upon my wrists. Still, I bear no grudge for that. It is all fair and above-board. If you want to hear my story I have no wish to hold it back. What I say to you is God's truth, every word of it. Thank you; you can put the glass beside me here, and I'll put my lips to it if I am dry.

"I am a Worcestershire man myself,—born near Pershore. I dare say you would find a heap of Smalls living there now if you were to look. I have often thought of taking a look round there, but the truth is that I was never much of a credit to the family, and I doubt if they would be so very glad to see me.

They were all steady, chapel-going folk, small farmers, well known and respected over the country-side, while I was always a bit of a rover. At last, however, when I was about eighteen, I gave them no more trouble, for I got into a mess over a girl, and could only get out of it again by taking the queen's shilling and joining the 3rd Buffs, which was just starting for India.

"I wasn't destined to do much soldiering, however. I had just got past the goose-step, and learned to handle my musket, when I was fool enough to go swimming in the Ganges. Luckily for me, my company sergeant, John Holder, was in the water at the same time, and he was one of the finest swimmers in the service. A crocodile took me, just as I was half-way across, and nipped off my right leg as clean as a surgeon could have done it, just above the knee. What with the shock and the loss of blood, I fainted, and should have drowned if Holder had not caught hold of me and paddled for the bank. I was five months in hospital over it, and when at last I was able to limp out of it with this timber toe strapped to my stump I found myself invalided out of the army and unfitted for any active occupation.

"I was, as you can imagine, pretty down on my luck at this time, for I was a useless cripple though not yet in my twentieth year. However, my misfortune soon proved to be a blessing in disguise. A man named Abelwhite, who had come out there as an indigo-planter, wanted an overseer to look after his coolies and keep them up to their work. He happened to be a friend of our colonel's, who had taken an interest in me since the accident. To make a long story short, the colonel recommended me strongly for the post and, as the work was mostly to be done on horseback, my leg was no great obstacle, for I had enough knee left to keep good grip on the saddle. What I had to do was to ride over the plantation, to keep an eye on the men as they worked, and to report the idlers. The pay was fair, I had comfortable quarters, and altogether I was content to spend the remainder of my life in indigo-planting. Mr. Abelwhite was a kind man, and he would often drop into my little shanty and smoke a pipe with me, for white folk out there feel their hearts warm to each other as they never do here at home.

"Well, I was never in luck's way long. Suddenly, without a note of warning, the great mutiny broke upon us. One month India lay as still and peaceful, to all appearance, as Surrey or Kent; the next there were two hundred thousand black devils let loose, and the country was a perfect hell. Of course you know all about it, gentlemen,—a deal more than I do, very like, since reading is not in my line. I only know what I saw with my own eyes. Our plantation was at a place called Muttra, near the border of the Northwest Provinces. Night after night the whole sky was alight with the burning bungalows, and day after day we had small companies of Europeans passing through our estate with their wives and children, on their way to Agra, where were the nearest troops. Mr. Abelwhite was an obstinate man. He had it in his head that the affair had been exaggerated, and that it would blow over as suddenly as it had sprung up. There he sat on his veranda, drinking whiskey-pegs and smoking cheroots, while the country was in a blaze about him. Of course we stuck by him, I and Dawson, who, with his wife, used to do the book-work and the managing. Well, one fine day the crash came. I had been away on a distant plantation, and was riding slowly home in the evening, when my eye fell upon something all huddled together at the bottom of a steep nullah. I rode down to see what it was, and the cold struck through my heart when I found it was Dawson's wife, all cut into ribbons, and half eaten by jackals and native dogs. A little further up the road Dawson himself was lying on his face, quite dead, with an empty revolver in his hand and four Sepoys lying across each other in front of him. I reined up my horse, wondering which way I should turn, but at that moment I saw thick smoke curling up from Abelwhite's bungalow and the flames beginning to burst through the roof. I knew then that I could do my employer no good, but would only throw my own life away if I meddled in the matter. From where I stood I could see hundreds of the black fiends, with their red coats still on their backs, dancing and howling round the burning house. Some of them pointed at me, and a couple of bullets sang past my head; so I broke away across the paddy-fields, and found myself late at night safe within the walls at Agra.

"As it proved, however, there was no great safety there, either. The whole country was up like a swarm of bees. Wherever the English could collect in little bands they held just the ground that their guns commanded. Everywhere else they were helpless fugitives. It was a fight of the millions against the hundreds; and the cruelest part of it was that these men that we fought against, foot, horse, and gunners, were our own picked troops, whom we had taught and trained, handling our own weapons, and blowing our own bugle-calls. At Agra there were the 3rd Bengal Fusiliers, some Sikhs, two troops of horse, and a battery of artillery. A volunteer corps of clerks and merchants had been formed, and this I joined, wooden leg and all. We went out to meet the rebels at Shahgunge early in July, and we beat them back for a time, but our powder gave out, and we had to fall back upon the city. Nothing but the worst news came to us from every side,—which is not to be wondered at, for if you look at the map you will see that we were right in the heart of it. Lucknow is rather better than a hundred miles to the east, and Cawnpore about as far to the south. From every point on the compass there was nothing but torture and murder and outrage.

"The city of Agra is a great place, swarming with fanatics and fierce devil-worshippers of all sorts. Our handful of men were lost among the narrow, winding streets. Our leader moved across the river, therefore, and took up his position in the old fort at Agra. I don't know if any of you gentlemen have ever read or heard anything of that old fort. It is a very queer place,—the queerest that ever I was in, and I have been in some rum corners, too. First of all, it is enormous in size. I should think that the enclosure must be acres and acres. There is a modern part, which took all our garrison, women, children, stores, and everything else, with plenty of room over. But the modern part is nothing like the size of the old quarter, where nobody goes, and which is given over to the scorpions and the centipedes. It is all full of great deserted halls, and winding passages, and long corridors twisting in and out, so that it is easy enough for folk to get lost in it. For this reason it was seldom that any one went into it, though now and again a party with torches might go exploring.

"The river washes along the front of the old fort, and so protects it, but on the sides and behind there are many doors, and these had to be guarded, of course, in the old quarter as well as in that which was actually held by our troops. We were short-handed, with hardly men enough to man the angles of the building and to serve the guns. It was impossible for us, therefore, to station a strong guard at every one of the innumerable gates. What we did was to organize a central guard-house in the middle of the fort, and to leave each gate under the charge of one white man and two or three natives. I was selected to take charge during certain hours of the night of a small isolated door upon the southwest side of the building. Two Sikh troopers were placed under my command,

and I was instructed if anything went wrong to fire my musket, when I might rely upon help coming at once from the central guard. As the guard was a good two hundred paces away, however, and as the space between was cut up into a labyrinth of passages and corridors, I had great doubts as to whether they could arrive in time to be of any use in case of an actual attack.

"Well, I was pretty proud at having this small command given me, since I was a raw recruit, and a game-legged one at that. For two nights I kept the watch with my Punjaubees. They were tall, fierce-looking chaps, Mahomet Singh and Abdullah Khan by name, both old fighting-men who had borne arms against us at Chilian-wallah. They could talk English pretty well, but I could get little out of them. They preferred to stand together and jabber all night in their queer Sikh lingo. For myself, I used to stand outside the gate-way, looking down on the broad, winding river and on the twinkling lights of the great city. The beating of drums, the rattle of tomtoms, and the yells and howls of the rebels, drunk with opium and with bang, were enough to remind us all night of our dangerous neighbors across the stream. Every two hours the officer of the night used to come round to all the posts, to make sure that all was well.

"The third night of my watch was dark and dirty, with a small, driving rain. It was dreary work standing in the gate-way hour after hour in such weather. I tried again and again to make my Sikhs talk, but without much success. At two in the morning the rounds passed, and broke for a moment the weariness of the night. Finding that my companions would not be led into conversation, I took out my pipe, and laid down my musket to strike the match. In an instant the two Sikhs were upon me. One of them snatched my firelock up and levelled it at my head, while the other held a great knife to my throat and swore between his teeth that he would plunge it into me if I moved a step.

"My first thought was that these fellows were in league with the rebels, and that this was the beginning of an assault. If our door were in the hands of the Sepoys the place must fall, and the women and children be treated as they were in Cawnpore. Maybe you gentlemen think that I am just making out a case for myself, but I give you my word that when I thought of that, though I felt the point of the knife at my throat, I opened my mouth with the intention of giving a scream, if it was my last one, which might alarm the main guard. The man who held me seemed to know my thoughts; for, even as I braced myself to it, he whispered, 'Don't make a noise. The fort is safe enough. There are no rebel dogs on this side of the river.' There was the ring of truth in what he said, and I knew that if I raised my voice I was a dead man. I could read it in the fellow's brown eyes. I waited, therefore, in silence, to see what it was that they wanted from me.

"'Listen to me, Sahib,' said the taller and fiercer of the pair, the one whom they called Abdullah Khan. 'You must either be with us now or you must be silenced forever. The thing is too great a one for us to hesitate. Either you are heart and soul with us on your oath on the cross of the Christians, or your body this night shall be thrown into the ditch and we shall pass over to our brothers in the rebel army. There is no middle way. Which is it to be, death or life? We can only give you three minutes to decide, for the time is passing, and all must be done before the rounds come again.'

"'How can I decide?' said I. 'You have not told me what you want of me. But I tell you now that if it is anything against the safety of the fort I will have no truck with it, so you can drive home your knife and welcome.'

"'It is nothing against the fort,' said he. 'We only ask you to do that which your countrymen come to this land for. We ask you to be rich. If you will be one of us this night, we will swear to you upon the naked knife, and by the threefold oath which no Sikh was ever known to break, that you shall have your fair share of the loot. A quarter of the treasure shall be yours. We can say no fairer.'

"'But what is the treasure, then?' I asked. 'I am as ready to be rich as you can be, if you will but show me how it can be done.'

"'You will swear, then,' said he, 'by the bones of your father, by the honor of your mother, by the cross of your faith, to raise no hand and speak no word against us, either now or afterwards?'

"'I will swear it,' I answered, 'provided that the fort is not endangered.'

"'Then my comrade and I will swear that you shall have a quarter of the treasure which shall be equally divided among the four of us.'

"'There are but three,' said I.

"'No; Dost Akbar must have his share. We can tell the tale to you while we await them. Do you stand at the gate, Mahomet Singh, and give notice of their coming. The thing stands thus, Sahib, and I tell it to you because I know that an oath is binding upon a Feringhee, and that we may trust you. Had you been a lying Hindu, though you had sworn by all the gods in their false temples, your blood would have been upon the knife, and your body in the water. But the Sikh knows the Englishman, and the Englishman knows the Sikh. Hearken, then, to what I have to say.

"'There is a rajah in the northern provinces who has much

wealth, though his lands are small. Much has come to him from his father, and more still he has set by himself, for he is of a low nature and hoards his gold rather than spend it. When the troubles broke out he would be friends both with the lion and the tiger,—with the Sepoy and with the Company's Raj. Soon, however, it seemed to him that the white men's day was come, for through all the land he could hear of nothing but of their death and their overthrow. Yet, being a careful man, he made such plans that, come what might, half at least of his treasure should be left to him. That which was in gold and silver he kept by him in the vaults of his palace, but the most precious stones and the choicest pearls that he had he put in an iron box, and sent it by a trusty servant who, under the guise of a merchant, should take it to the fort at Agra, there to lie until the land is at peace. Thus, if the rebels won he would have his money, but if the Company conquered his jewels would be saved to him. Having thus divided his hoard, he threw himself into the cause of the Sepoys, since they were strong upon his borders. By doing this, mark you, Sahib, his property becomes the due of those who have been true to their salt.

"'This pretended merchant, who travels under the name of Achmet, is now in the city of Agra, and desires to gain his way into the fort. He has with him as travelling-companion my foster-brother Dost Akbar, who knows his secret. Dost Akbar has promised this night to lead him to a side-postern of the fort, and has chosen this one for his purpose. Here he will come presently, and here he will find Mahomet Singh and myself awaiting him. The place is lonely, and none shall know of his coming. The world shall know of the merchant Achmet no more, but the great treasure of the rajah shall be divided among us. What say you to it, Sahib?'

"In Worcestershire the life of a man seems a great and a

sacred thing; but it is very different when there is fire and blood all round you and you have been used to meeting death at every turn. Whether Achmet the merchant lived or died was a thing as light as air to me, but at the talk about the treasure my heart turned to it, and I thought of what I might do in the old country with it, and how my folk would stare when they saw their ne'er-do-well coming back with his pockets full of gold moidores. I had, therefore, already made up my mind. Abdullah Khan, however, thinking that I hesitated, pressed the matter more closely.

"'Consider, Sahib,' said he, 'that if this man is taken by the commandant he will be hung or shot, and his jewels taken by the government, so that no man will be a rupee the better for them. Now, since we do the taking of him, why should we not do the rest as well? The jewels will be as well with us as in the Company's coffers. There will be enough to make every one of us rich men and great chiefs. No one can know about the matter, for here we are cut off from all men. What could be better for the purpose? Say again, then, Sahib, whether you are with us, or if we must look upon you as an enemy.'

"'I am with you heart and soul,' said I.

"'It is well,' he answered, handing me back my firelock. 'You see that we trust you, for your word, like ours, is not to be broken. We have now only to wait for my brother and the merchant.'

"'Does your brother know, then, of what you will do?' I asked.

"'The plan is his. He has devised it. We will go to the gate and share the watch with Mahomet Singh.'

"The rain was still falling steadily, for it was just the beginning of the wet season. Brown, heavy clouds were drifting across the sky, and it was hard to see more than a stone-cast. A deep moat lay in front of our door, but the water was in places nearly dried up, and it could easily be crossed. It was strange to me to be standing there with those two wild Punjaubees waiting for the man who was coming to his death.

"Suddenly my eye caught the glint of a shaded lantern at the other side of the moat. It vanished among the mound-heaps, and then appeared again coming slowly in our direction.

"'Here they are!' I exclaimed.

"'You will challenge him, Sahib, as usual,' whispered Abdullah. 'Give him no cause for fear. Send us in with him, and we shall do the rest while you stay here on guard. Have the lantern ready to uncover, that we may be sure that it is indeed the man.'

"The light had flickered onwards, now stopping and now advancing, until I could see two dark figures upon the other side of the moat. I let them scramble down the sloping bank, splash through the mire, and climb half-way up to the gate, before I challenged them.

"'Who goes there?' said I, in a subdued voice.

"'Friends,' came the answer. I uncovered my lantern and threw a flood of light upon them. The first was an enormous Sikh, with a black beard which swept nearly down to his cummerbund. Outside of a show I have never seen so tall a man. The other was a little, fat, round fellow, with a great yellow turban, and a bundle in his hand, done up in a shawl. He seemed to be all in a quiver with fear, for his hands twitched as if he had the ague, and his head kept turning to left and right with two bright little twinkling eyes, like a mouse when he ventures out from his hole. It gave me the chills to think of killing him, but I thought of the treasure, and my heart set as hard as a flint within me. When he saw my white face he gave a little chirrup of joy and came running up towards me.

"'Your protection, Sahib,' he panted,—'your protection for the unhappy merchant Achmet. I have travelled across Rajpootana that I might seek the shelter of the fort at Agra. I have been robbed and beaten and abused because I have been the friend of the Company. It is a blessed night this when I am once more in safety,—I and my poor possessions.'

"'What have you in the bundle?' I asked.

"'An iron box,' he answered, 'which contains one or two little family matters which are of no value to others, but which I should be sorry to lose. Yet I am not a beggar; and I shall reward you, young Sahib, and your governor also, if he will give me the shelter I ask.'

"I could not trust myself to speak longer with the man. The more I looked at his fat, frightened face, the harder did it seem that we should slay him in cold blood. It was best to get it over.

"'Take him to the main guard,' said I. The two Sikhs closed in upon him on each side, and the giant walked behind, while they marched in through the dark gate-way. Never was a man so compassed round with death. I remained at the gate-way with the lantern.

"I could hear the measured tramp of their footsteps sounding through the lonely corridors. Suddenly it ceased, and I heard voices, and a scuffle, with the sound of blows. A moment later there came, to my horror, a rush of footsteps coming in my direction, with the loud breathing of a running man. I turned my lantern down the long, straight passage, and there was the fat man, running like the wind, with a smear of blood across his face, and close at his heels, bounding like a tiger, the great black-bearded Sikh, with a knife flashing in his hand. I have never seen a man run so fast as that little merchant. He was gaining on the Sikh, and I could see that if he once passed me and got to the open air he would save himself yet. My heart softened to him, but again the thought of his treasure turned me hard and bitter. I cast my firelock between his legs as he raced past, and he rolled twice over like a shot rabbit. Ere he could stagger to his feet the Sikh was upon him, and buried his knife twice in his side. The man never uttered moan nor moved muscle, but lay were he had fallen. I think myself that he may have broken his neck with the fall. You see, gentlemen, that I am keeping my promise. I am telling you every work of the business just exactly as it happened, whether it is in my favor or not."

He stopped, and held out his manacled hands for the whiskey-and-water which Holmes had brewed for him. For myself, I confess that I had now conceived the utmost horror of the man, not only for this cold-blooded business in which he had been concerned, but even more for the somewhat flippant and careless way in which he narrated it. Whatever punishment was in store for him, I felt that he might expect no sympathy from me. Sherlock Holmes and Jones sat with their hands upon their knees, deeply interested in the story, but with the same disgust written upon their faces. He may have observed it, for there was a touch of defiance in his voice and manner as he proceeded.

"It was all very bad, no doubt," said he. "I should like to know how many fellows in my shoes would have refused a share of this loot when they knew that they would have their throats cut for their pains. Besides, it was my life or his when once he was in the fort. If he had got out, the whole business

233

would come to light, and I should have been court-martialed and shot as likely as not;   for people were not very lenient at a time like that."

"Go on with your story," said Holmes, shortly.

"Well, we carried him in, Abdullah, Akbar, and I. A fine weight he was, too, for all that he was so short. Mahomet Singh was left to guard the door. We took him to a place which the Sikhs had already prepared. It was some distance off, where a winding passage leads to a great empty hall, the brick walls of which were all crumbling to pieces. The earth floor had sunk in at one place, making a natural grave, so we left Achmet the merchant there, having first covered him over with loose bricks. This done, we all went back to the treasure.

"It lay where he had dropped it when he was first attacked. The box was the same which now lies open upon your table. A key was hung by a silken cord to that carved handle upon the top. We opened it, and the light of the lantern gleamed upon a collection of gems such as I have read of and thought about when I was a little lad at Pershore. It was blinding to look upon them. When we had feasted our eyes we took them all out and made a list of them. There were one hundred and forty-three diamonds of the first water, including one which has been called, I believe, 'the Great Mogul' and is said to be the second largest stone in existence. Then there were ninety-seven very fine emeralds, and one hundred and seventy rubies, some of which, however, were small. There were forty carbuncles, two hundred and ten sapphires, sixty-one agates, and a great quantity of beryls, onyxes, cats'-eyes, turquoises, and other stones, the very names of which I did not know at the time, though I have become more familiar with them since. Besides this, there were nearly three hundred very fine pearls, twelve of which were set in a gold coronet. By the way, these last had been taken out of the chest and were not there when I recovered it.

"After we had counted our treasures we put them back into the chest and carried them to the gate-way to show them to Mahomet Singh. Then we solemnly renewed our oath to stand by each other and be true to our secret. We agreed to conceal our loot in a safe place until the country should be at peace again, and then to divide it equally among ourselves. There was no use dividing it at present, for if gems of such value were found upon us it would cause suspicion, and there was no privacy in the fort nor any place where we could keep them. We carried the box, therefore, into the same hall where we had buried the body, and there, under certain bricks in the best-preserved wall, we made a hollow and put our treasure. We made careful note of the place, and next day I drew four plans, one for each of us, and put the sign of the four of us at the bottom, for we had sworn that we should each always act for all, so that none might take advantage. That is an oath that I can put my hand to my heart and swear that I have never broken.

"Well, there's no use my telling you gentlemen what came of the Indian mutiny. After Wilson took Delhi and Sir Colin relieved Lucknow the back of the business was broken. Fresh troops came pouring in, and Nana Sahib made himself scarce over the frontier. A flying column under Colonel Greathed came round to Agra and cleared the Pandies away from it. Peace seemed to be settling upon the country, and we four were beginning to hope that the time was at hand when we might safely go off with our shares of the plunder. In a moment, however, our hopes were shattered by our being arrested as the murderers of Achmet.

"It came about in this way. When the rajah put his jewels

into the hands of Achmet he did it because he knew that he was a trusty man. They are suspicious folk in the East, however: so what does this rajah do but take a second even more trusty servant and set him to play the spy upon the first? This second man was ordered never to let Achmet out of his sight, and he followed him like his shadow. He went after him that night and saw him pass through the doorway. Of course he thought he had taken refuge in the fort, and applied for admission there himself next day, but could find no trace of Achmet. This seemed to him so strange that he spoke about it to a sergeant of guides, who brought it to the ears of the commandant. A thorough search was quickly made, and the body was discovered. Thus at the very moment that we thought that all was safe we were all four seized and brought to trial on a charge of murder,—three of us because we had held the gate that night, and the fourth because he was known to have been in the company of the murdered man. Not a word about the jewels came out at the trial, for the rajah had been deposed and driven out of India: so no one had any particular interest in them. The murder, however, was clearly made out, and it was certain that we must all have been concerned in it. The three Sikhs got penal servitude for life, and I was condemned to death, though my sentence was afterwards commuted into the same as the others.

"It was rather a queer position that we found ourselves in then. There we were all four tied by the leg and with precious little chance of ever getting out again, while we each held a secret which might have put each of us in a palace if we could only have made use of it. It was enough to make a man eat his heart out to have to stand the kick and the cuff of every petty jack-in-office, to have rice to eat and water to drink, when that gorgeous fortune was ready for him outside, just waiting to be picked up. It might have driven me mad; but I was always a pretty stubborn one, so I just held on and bided my time.

"At last it seemed to me to have come. I was changed from Agra to Madras, and from there to Blair Island in the Andamans. There are very few white convicts at this settlement, and, as I had behaved well from the first, I soon found myself a sort of privileged person. I was given a hut in Hope Town, which is a small place on the slopes of Mount Harriet, and I was left pretty much to myself. It is a dreary, fever-stricken place, and all beyond our little clearings was infested with wild cannibal natives, who were ready enough to blow a poisoned dart at us if they saw a chance. There was digging, and ditching, and yam-planting, and a dozen other things to be done, so we were busy enough all day;   though in the evening we had a little time to ourselves. Among other things, I learned to dispense drugs for the surgeon, and picked up a smattering of his knowledge. All the time I was on the lookout for a chance of escape;   but it is hundreds of miles from any other land, and there is little or no wind in those seas: so it was a terribly difficult job to get away.

"The surgeon, Dr. Somerton, was a fast, sporting young chap, and the other young officers would meet in his rooms of an evening and play cards. The surgery, where I used to make up my drugs, was next to his sitting-room, with a small window between us. Often, if I felt lonesome, I used to turn out the lamp in the surgery, and then, standing there, I could hear their talk and watch their play. I am fond of a hand at cards myself, and it was almost as good as having one to watch the others. There was Major Sholto, Captain Morstan, and Lieutenant Bromley Brown, who were in command of the native troops, and there was the surgeon himself, and two or three prison-officials, crafty old hands who played a nice sly safe game. A very snug little party they used to make.

"Well, there was one thing which very soon struck me, and that was that the soldiers used always to lose and the civilians to win. Mind, I don't say that there was anything unfair, but so it was. These prison-chaps had done little else than play cards ever since they had been at the Andamans, and they knew each other's game to a point, while the others just played to pass the time and threw their cards down anyhow. Night after night the soldiers got up poorer men, and the poorer they got the more keen they were to play. Major Sholto was the hardest hit. He used to pay in notes and gold at first, but soon it came to notes of hand and for big sums. He sometimes would win for a few deals, just to give him heart, and then the luck would set in against him worse than ever. All day he would wander about as black as thunder, and he took to drinking a deal more than was good for him.

"One night he lost even more heavily than usual. I was sitting in my hut when he and Captain Morstan came stumbling along on the way to their quarters. They were bosom friends, those two, and never far apart. The major was raving about his losses.

"'It's all up, Morstan,' he was saying, as they passed my hut. 'I shall have to send in my papers. I am a ruined man.'

"'Nonsense, old chap!' said the other, slapping him upon the shoulder. 'I've had a nasty facer myself, but—' That was all I could hear, but it was enough to set me thinking.

"A couple of days later Major Sholto was strolling on the beach: so I took the chance of speaking to him.

"'I wish to have your advice, major,' said I.

"'Well, Small, what is it?' he asked, taking his cheroot from his lips.

"'I wanted to ask you, sir,' said I, 'who is the proper

person to whom hidden treasure should be handed over. I know where half a million worth lies, and, as I cannot use it myself, I thought perhaps the best thing that I could do would be to hand it over to the proper authorities, and then perhaps they would get my sentence shortened for me.'

"'Half a million, Small?' he gasped, looking hard at me to see if I was in earnest.

"'Quite that, sir,—in jewels and pearls. It lies there ready for any one. And the queer thing about it is that the real owner is outlawed and cannot hold property, so that it belongs to the first comer.'

"'To government, Small,' he stammered,—'to government.' But he said it in a halting fashion, and I knew in my heart that I had got him.

"'You think, then, sir, that I should give the information to the Governor-General?' said I, quietly.

"'Well, well, you must not do anything rash, or that you might repent. Let me hear all about it, Small. Give me the facts.'

"I told him the whole story, with small changes so that he could not identify the places. When I had finished he stood stock still and full of thought. I could see by the twitch of his lip that there was a struggle going on within him.

"'This is a very important matter, Small,' he said, at last. 'You must not say a word to any one about it, and I shall see you again soon.'

"Two nights later he and his friend Captain Morstan came to my hut in the dead of the night with a lantern.

"'I want you just to let Captain Morstan hear that story from your own lips, Small,' said he.

"I repeated it as I had told it before.

"'It rings true, eh?' said he. 'It's good enough to act upon?'

"Captain Morstan nodded.

"'Look here, Small,' said the major. 'We have been talking it over, my friend here and I, and we have come to the conclusion that this secret of yours is hardly a government matter, after all, but is a private concern of your own, which of course you have the power of disposing of as you think best. Now, the question is, what price would you ask for it? We might be inclined to take it up, and at least look into it, if we could agree as to terms.' He tried to speak in a cool, careless way, but his eyes were shining with excitement and greed.

"'Why, as to that, gentlemen,' I answered, trying also to be cool, but feeling as excited as he did, 'there is only one bargain which a man in my position can make. I shall want you to help me to my freedom, and to help my three companions to theirs. We shall then take you into partnership, and give you a fifth share to divide between you.'

"'Hum!' said he. 'A fifth share! That is not very tempting.'

"'It would come to fifty thousand apiece,' said I.

"'But how can we gain your freedom? You know very well that you ask an impossibility.'

"'Nothing of the sort,' I answered. 'I have thought it all out to the last detail. The only bar to our escape is that we can get no boat fit for the voyage, and no provisions to last us for so long a time. There are plenty of little yachts and yawls at Calcutta or Madras which would serve our turn well. Do you bring one over. We shall engage to get aboard her by night, and if you will drop us on any part of the Indian coast you will have done your part of the bargain.'

"'If there were only one,' he said.

"'None or all,' I answered. 'We have sworn it. The four of us must always act together.'

"'You see, Morstan,' said he, 'Small is a man of his word. He does not flinch from his friend. I think we may very well trust him.'

"'It's a dirty business,' the other answered. 'Yet, as you say, the money would save our commissions handsomely.'

"'Well, Small,' said the major, 'we must, I suppose, try and meet you. We must first, of course, test the truth of your story. Tell me where the box is hid, and I shall get leave of absence and go back to India in the monthly relief-boat to inquire into the affair.'

"'Not so fast,' said I, growing colder as he got hot. 'I must have the consent of my three comrades. I tell you that it is four or none with us.'

"'Nonsense!' he broke in. 'What have three black fellows to do with our agreement?'

"'Black or blue,' said I, 'they are in with me, and we all go together.'

"Well, the matter ended by a second meeting, at which Mahomet Singh, Abdullah Khan, and Dost Akbar were all present. We talked the matter over again, and at last we came to an arrangement. We were to provide both the officers with charts of the part of the Agra fort and mark the place in the wall where the treasure was hid. Major Sholto was to go to India to test our story. If he found the box he was to leave it there, to send out a small yacht provisioned for a voyage, which was to lie off Rutland Island, and to which we were to make our way, and finally to return to his duties. Captain Morstan was then to apply for leave of absence, to meet us at Agra, and there we were to have a final division of the treasure, he taking the major's share as well as his own. All this we sealed by the most solemn oaths that the mind could think or the lips utter. I sat up all night with paper and ink, and by the morning I had the two charts all ready, signed with the sign of four,—that is, of Abdullah, Akbar, Mahomet, and myself.

"Well, gentlemen, I weary you with my long story, and I know that my friend Mr. Jones is impatient to get me safely stowed in chokey. I'll make it as short as I can. The villain Sholto went off to India, but he never came back again. Captain Morstan showed me his name among a list of passengers in one of the mail-boats very shortly afterwards. His uncle had died, leaving him a fortune, and he had left the army, yet he could stoop to treat five men as he had treated us. Morstan went over to Agra shortly afterwards, and found, as we expected, that the treasure was indeed gone. The scoundrel had stolen it all, without carrying out one of the conditions on which we had sold him the secret. From that day I lived only for vengeance. I thought of it by day and I nursed it by night. It became an overpowering, absorbing passion with me. I cared nothing for the law,—nothing for the gallows. To escape, to track down Sholto, to have my hand upon his throat,—that was my one thought. Even the Agra treasure had come to be a smaller thing in my mind than the slaying of Sholto.

"Well, I have set my mind on many things in this life, and never one which I did not carry out. But it was weary years before my time came. I have told you that I had picked up something of medicine. One day when Dr. Somerton was down with a fever a little Andaman Islander was picked up by a convict-gang in the woods. He was sick to death, and had gone to a lonely place to die. I took him in hand, though he was as venomous as a young snake, and after a couple of months I got him all right and able to walk. He took a kind of fancy to me then, and would hardly go back to his woods, but was always hanging about my hut. I learned a little of his lingo from him, and this made him all the fonder of me.

"Tonga—for that was his name—was a fine boatman, and owned a big, roomy canoe of his own. When I found that he was devoted to me and would do anything to serve me, I saw my chance of escape. I talked it over with him. He was to bring his boat round on a certain night to an old wharf which was never guarded, and there he was to pick me up. I gave him directions to have several gourds of water and a lot of yams, cocoa-nuts, and sweet potatoes.

"He was stanch and true, was little Tonga. No man ever had a more faithful mate. At the night named he had his boat at the wharf. As it chanced, however, there was one of the convict-guard down there,—a vile Pathan who had never missed a chance of insulting and injuring me. I had always vowed vengeance, and now I had my chance. It was as if fate had placed him in my way that I might pay my debt before I left the island. He stood on the bank with his back to me, and his carbine on his shoulder. I looked about for a stone to beat out his brains with, but none could I see. Then a queer thought came into my head and showed me where I could lay my hand on a weapon. I sat down in the darkness and unstrapped my wooden leg. With three long hops I was on him. He put his carbine to his shoulder, but I struck him full, and knocked the whole front of his skull in. You can see the split in the wood now where I hit him. We both went down together, for I could not keep my balance, but when I got up I found him still lying quiet enough. I made for the boat, and in an hour we were well out at sea. Tonga had brought all his earthly possessions with him, his arms and his gods. Among other things, he had a long bamboo spear, and some Andaman cocoa-nut matting, with which I made a sort of sail. For ten days we were beating about, trusting to luck, and on the eleventh we were picked up by a trader which was going from Singapore to Jiddah with a cargo of Malay pilgrims. They were a rum crowd, and Tonga and I soon managed to settle down among them. They had one very good quality: they let you alone and asked no questions.

"Well, if I were to tell you all the adventures that my little chum and I went through, you would not thank me, for I would have you here until the sun was shining. Here and there we drifted about the world, something always turning up to keep us from London. All the time, however, I never lost sight of my purpose. I would dream of Sholto at night. A hundred times I have killed him in my sleep. At last, however, some three or four years ago, we found ourselves in England. I had no great difficulty in finding where Sholto lived, and I set to work to discover whether he had realized the treasure, or if he still had it. I made friends with someone who could help me,—I name no names, for I don't want to get any one else in a hole,—and I soon found that he still had the jewels. Then I tried to get at him in many ways; but he was pretty sly, and had always two prize-fighters, besides his sons and his khitmutgar, on guard over him.

"One day, however, I got word that he was dying. I hurried at once to the garden, mad that he should slip out of my clutches like that, and, looking through the window, I saw him lying in his bed, with his sons on each side of him. I'd have come through and taken my chance with the three of them, only even as I looked at him his jaw dropped, and I knew that he was gone. I got into his room that same night, though, and I searched his papers to see if there was any record of where he had hidden our jewels. There was not a line, however: so I came away, bitter and savage as a man could be. Before I left I bethought me that if I ever met my Sikh friends again it would be a satisfaction to know that I had left some mark of our hatred: so I scrawled down the sign of the four of us, as it had been on the chart, and I pinned it on his bosom. It was too much that he should be taken to the grave without some token from the men whom he had robbed and befooled.

"We earned a living at this time by my exhibiting poor Tonga at fairs and other such places as the black cannibal. He would eat raw meat and dance his war-dance: so we always had a hatful of pennies after a day's work. I still heard all the news from Pondicherry Lodge, and for some years there was no news to hear, except that they were hunting for the treasure. At last, however, came what we had waited for so long. The treasure had been found. It was up at the top of the house, in Mr. Bartholomew Sholto's chemical laboratory. I came at once and had a look at the place, but I could not see how with my wooden leg I was to make my way up to it. I learned, however, about a trap-door in the roof, and also about Mr. Sholto's supper-hour. It seemed to me that I could manage the thing easily through Tonga. I brought him out with me with a long rope wound round his waist. He could climb like a cat, and he soon made his way through the roof, but, as ill luck would have it, Bartholomew Sholto was still in the room, to his cost. Tonga thought he had done something very clever in killing him, for when I came up by the rope I found him strutting about as proud as a peacock. Very much surprised was he when I made at him with the rope's end and cursed him for a little blood-thirsty imp. I took the treasure-box and let it down, and then slid down myself, having first left the sign of the four upon the table, to show that the jewels had come back at last to those who had most right to them. Tonga then pulled up the rope, closed the window, and made off the way that he had come.

"I don't know that I have anything else to tell you. I had heard a waterman speak of the speed of Smith's launch the Aurora, so I thought she would be a handy craft for our escape. I engaged with old Smith, and was to give him a big sum if he got us safe to our ship. He knew, no doubt, that there was some screw loose, but he was not in our secrets. All this is the truth, and if I tell it to you, gentlemen, it is not to amuse you,—for you have not done me a very good turn,—but it is because I believe the best defense I can make is just to hold back nothing, but let all the world know how badly I have myself been served by Major Sholto, and how innocent I am of the death of his son."

"A very remarkable account," said Sherlock Holmes. "A fitting wind-up to an extremely interesting case. There is nothing at all new to me in the latter part of your narrative, except that you brought your own rope. That I did not know. By the way, I had hoped that Tonga had lost all his darts; yet he managed to shoot one at us in the boat."

"He had lost them all, sir, except the one which was in his blow-pipe at the time."

"Ah, of course," said Holmes. "I had not thought of that."

"Is there any other point which you would like to ask about?" asked the convict, affably.

"I think not, thank you," my companion answered.

"Well, Holmes," said Athelney Jones, "You are a man to be humored, and we all know that you are a connoisseur of crime, but duty is duty, and I have gone rather far in doing what you and your friend asked me. I shall feel more at ease when we have our story-teller here safe under lock and key. The cab still waits, and there are two inspectors down-stairs. I am much obliged to you both for your assistance. Of course you will be wanted at the trial. Good-night to you."

"Good-night, gentlemen both," said Jonathan Small.

"You first, Small," remarked the wary Jones as they left the room. "I'll take particular care that you don't club me with your wooden leg, whatever you may have done to the gentleman at the Andaman Isles."

"Well, and there is the end of our little drama," I remarked, after we had set some time smoking in silence. "I fear that it may be the last investigation in which I shall have the chance of studying your methods. Miss Morstan has done me the honor to accept me as a husband in prospective."

He gave a most dismal groan. "I feared as much," said he. "I really cannot congratulate you."

I was a little hurt. "Have you any reason to be dissatisfied with my choice?" I asked.

"Not at all. I think she is one of the most charming young ladies I ever met, and might have been most useful in such work as we have been doing. She had a decided genius that way: witness the way in which she preserved that Agra plan from all the other papers of her father. But love is an emotional thing, and whatever is emotional is opposed to that true cold reason which I place above all things. I should never marry myself, lest I bias my judgment."

"I trust," said I, laughing, "that my judgment may survive the ordeal. But you look weary."

"Yes, the reaction is already upon me. I shall be as limp as a rag for a week."

"Strange," said I, "how terms of what in another man I should call laziness alternate with your fits of splendid energy and vigor."

"Yes," he answered, "there are in me the makings of a very fine loafer and also of a pretty spry sort of fellow. I often think of those lines of old Goethe,—

Schade dass die Natur nur EINEN Mensch aus Dir schuf,
Denn zum wuerdigen Mann war und zum Schelmen der Stoff.

"By the way, a propos of this Norwood business, you see that they had, as I surmised, a confederate in the house, who could be none other than Lal Rao, the butler: so Jones actually has the undivided honor of having caught one fish in his great haul."

"The division seems rather unfair," I remarked. "You have done all the work in this business. I get a wife out of it, Jones gets the credit, pray what remains for you?"

"For me," said Sherlock Holmes, "there still remains the cocaine-bottle." And he stretched his long white hand up for it.

Made in the USA
Middletown, DE
11 November 2018